CLANDESTINE

V. J. Spencer

For Shannon
My very own Bella Lockett

CLANDESTINE (ADJ.)

Kept secret or done secretively, especially describing something which is unlawful or not officially allowed.

BEFORE

MANDATORY (ADJ.)

A compulsory action; required by law. Without dispute.

I do not believe any of them wanted to go. No one appeared excited here, from what my research has shown. Any statements in the press from young cadets about the hopes they had for their shining futures were most likely propaganda. Yet this was what had to be done, regardless. This was the next step on their educational conveyor belt. Older siblings had done this before them, including Nia's older brother, and her parents, and theirs. This was what was done, in those days. What made it scary for the new recruits, however, was how little they had been told about the experiences yet to come. Their own families, their own parents would go silent on the subject if ever they were asked. The secrecy was unsettling.

CHAPTER ONE

128 DAYS BEFORE

They were ankle-deep in water by the time the bus arrived to pick them up. Despite wearing leather boots that covered her up to her knees, Nia was still soaked to the skin and shivering amongst the rest. The rain continued to beat down upon them ceaselessly. Their clothes, their conversations and their hearts had given up on the bus ever arriving. But they were too terrified of what would happen if they attempted to go back home.

The grey street was imprisoned by its grey buildings, which stretched upwards to the ever-grey sky. It filled Nia's heart with a sad, submissive ache. The water began to fill her boots. It made them squint as they looked at one another, oblivious; hopelessly searching for an answer to the questions they were all thinking: *Why are we here? What is the point?*

They knew only one thing for certain: they could not go home.

Not now, not as the same cowardly people who had left an hour before.

Their excuses would do no good. They were still only children. But still, it made no difference.

Despite their age, Nia noticed in the eyes around her that the world had encouraged them to grow up too fast. This accelerated childhood had stretched the skin over their bones and drained the smiles from their faces. Replacing their youthful, joyful eyes with those of the common rush-hour folk – that look so often seen on the underground trains early in the morning, accompanied by a sturdy briefcase in one hand and a shimmering, commanding screen in the other.

The message was clear: the adults go to work and so they must also. There was always so much to do, and so everyone must always be working. There is a goal, you see. Nobody seems to know what it is, or where the finish line can be found. But there is a goal, and they knew they must work towards it.

The only flaw that Nia could see within this theory was that most people died before they got there. Perhaps they just didn't run fast enough. Perhaps they simply lost their way with all their speed, no longer able to find their way back to the path. No one really knew.

Those kids – there in the rain – they were nearing the final stage of education before they took their place in the grand, mechanical way of living. That is why they waited, with no complaint. That was the way they had been trained.

A great roar of a motor signalled the arrival of the bus. One of them held out their arm to signal it to stop. It was going to regardless, due to the amount of wet people stood huddled under the rusting sign:

CONSCRIPTION CADETS: PICK-UP POINT 6

Then, each in an orderly fashion, one by one, they stepped onto the vehicle and exchanged a single large copper coin for the privilege of getting out of the rain. Some of them were fortunate enough to get a seat. Others were not so lucky. They had to stand and shiver a while longer yet.

The doors slid closed with a mournful whine. It was the only sound on the bus. The driver looked blankly ahead as he followed his memorised routine. The air inside felt thick, and the windows turned cloudy from the warmth of the sardined bodies. Black puffs of dirtied air coughed and wheezed out of the back of the long vehicle and into the surrounding world. Nia watched it rise and disappear through the window. She wondered if it was really gone.

Surrounding her were bodies that were steadily regaining heat, their clothes drip-drying as they hung off their bones. If it weren't for the dampness, they would all have looked rather smart. This was, after all, an important journey they were embarking on today. So they were told, at least.

Beside Nia sat her cousin, Jay. He was a young man of a similar age to Nia. He had floppy caramel curls and a sly smile, on the few occasions that it ever appeared at the corners of his tightly shut mouth. Nia felt fortunate that she had someone beside her through all of this. They had been the best of friends since childhood. Whenever they could sneak away, they had frequently enjoyed playing in the woods together. It was a way to forget the seriousness that surrounded the rest of their lives.

As children, they had an escape. As eighteen-year-olds, they did not.

That morning, when they had closed their suitcases and their bedroom doors for what would be the final time, they had shared a very brief moment in the upstairs corridor of the house. All had been still. The clock ticked away quietly to itself on the landing and they had closed their respective doors almost in unison. Nia looked at Jay, and Jay looked at Nia, and each of them had shared the same expression. The unmistakable combination of fear, nerves, and nausea.

It was common knowledge, back then. It happened for everyone. The two people who were leaving that house that day would not be the same two people who returned, three years from now – if they ever returned at all.

Without warning, Jay had pulled Nia into an embrace. He encased her. She was struck by how tall he now was. In her eyes, he was still the mischievous kid he had been when they grew up. To him, Nia was still the little blonde girl who had found joy in pointless trinkets like old pennies. That was what it felt like, for that brief moment, as they clung onto one another.

It was the childhood friends within them saying goodbye.

CHILDHOOD (N.)

The state or period of life in which a human is a child, often associated with memories of fun and happiness upon reflection in later life.
See also: NOSTALGIA and LABOUR.

In those days, life turned like a mechanical wheel: disciplined, rigid and monotonous. Children were raised strictly, under the same schooling, the same rules, and the same life plan as their peers, constructed before them from the moment they were born. This plan was not optional. Deviances were not tolerated. Questions were not asked, and – if they *were* – answers were not given. Everyone made the mistake of sticking with the same, stagnant excuse: this is the way we have always done it, for as long as we can remember.

This parasitic way of thinking resulted in an entire population who very rarely asked the question *why?*. A passive, entirely authority-driven society. You or I might call it a dictatorship. Explanations were few and far between; and if it was a question that could be answered, it was done so with the assumption that further questioning would not be needed.

This matter was particularly true of anything to do with the Government. Nobody knew anything – not for a *fact* – about the way the country was run. The Government very rarely spoke to the people directly. The people were kept satisfactorily happy. According to the Authorities, and the Dictator, the people had no need to speak with them at all – nor the right to.

"Here is the Life Plan of every individual that exists, and ever will exist."

Education, work, housing, transportation, marital partners. All was mostly predetermined for them. And, believe it or not, for a fair bit of time, it worked.

The only choice they received in their life was their career.

Once they chose, there was no turning back. Straying was punishable by death. Those who strayed or rebelled were outcasts, publicly shamed – never seen or spoken of again.

CHAPTER TWO

128 DAYS BEFORE

Nia looked left and right along the train station platform. Either side of her, in a perfect, orderly line, stood the rest of the people her age who would soon be taking the same journey she was. The line stretched for what seemed like miles. She couldn't see the end of it. She wondered what the others were thinking and wondered if it was all the same: whether they were all as similar on the inside as they appeared on the outside.

Each of the women wore dresses that covered their knees, all in a similar style, and of various Governmental-approved colours. Over that, a woollen coat, with circular buttons in the same colour as the wool. They always wore dark shoes; brown or black, and a beret cap to match. Some were not wearing them today. Nia was too scared not to and preferred how it disguised the back of her head. Being slightly taller than the average female she was somewhat self-conscious today of how she looked.

The clothes were comfortable, practical and fashionable for the time. Truth be told, most of them did feel very smart as they walked, and most certainly wanted to blend in with the rest, terrified at the prospect of standing out. What did help, of course, was that everyone around her had also been caught in the rain. Nia's coat, not being resistant to the water, felt uncomfortably sticky. *It is the fine rain that soaks you through*, as her grandfather would say - his response for every negative situation.

Shortly after an announcement over the speakers, the train steadily pulled in front of them all. It was as long and infinite as the platform itself, or so it seemed, and shone a glistening and gleaming crimson red. As a child, Nia had heard rumours about this train. On the schoolyard, people had whispered that it was painted by the blood of those cadets who did not make it home.

Still, no one appeared keen. Usual daily commutes to the offices or to school would consist of people bustling hurriedly, as politely as possible, all eager to be the first to step on board. Here, nobody moved for an awfully long time.

> And who can blame them? They did not wish to go. They did not wish to grow up.

Remarkably, as if they knew the crowd they would be faced with, the doors opened, all at once, all along the platform. Behind each sliding door stood a welcoming figure. A conductor, of sorts. Some men, some ladies, all smiling as if this was the day they had waited their entire lives for – and the expectation was that the children, too, should do the same.

"Welcome, welcome!" they said, as they ushered the passengers onto the train. In front of Nia stood a small but orderly line that had emerged from the crowd. She realised she was standing in line, and it had begun to form around her. Behind, she heard whispers and mutterings. She tried to believe they were not whispering about her or her family. She gulped. Part of her wondered why there was a universal aura of anxiety and resistance. They were scared, undoubtedly, but what was it they feared?

> What indeed… this is something I find so remarkable about humanity: if we decide to listen to our gut, and I mean really listen, we can know such remarkable things while simultaneously not knowing anything at all. Nia felt scared but did not know why. It was her gut talking to her. It made her knees tremble and the tips of her fingers went numb and cold. Her gut knew. It was trying to tell her something. But Nia herself was tricked by the

fact that the gentleman she was quickly approaching appeared nothing but polite and welcoming. She was trusting to her eyes, not her gut; and that, I tell you, is always a big mistake.

"And what is your name, ma'am?" he asked, when she was suddenly presented at the front of the line.

"Galloway, Ardenia."

"Ah, yes, here you are." He looked down at a tablet he held in his hand. Nia noticed he held her entire life history and personal information balanced on one palm. Her existence had been condensed down onto a single rectangle of artificial life. A rectangle so intelligent that it could recognise her from her voice, when the human man in front of her could not.

"When you step on board, turn left, and find the seat with your name on it. We've reserved it especially for you."

He gave her another winning smile. A smirk that you would expect to see from an amused gentleman at a dinner party. As Nia followed his instructions, she couldn't help but find his manner rather endearing. She began to relax. Lulled into a sudden sense of security.

The train carriage was not like those she had seen before. Nia had expected the conventional rows of paired seats, separated by an aisle, with windows to gaze out of when one's mind fancied a wander. This train gave no such things. Despite nearly twenty people boarding the carriage before her, she could not see a row of heads, as she had expected. Instead of seats, there were rows of singular black doors. They looked as if they were made of marble: polished and gleaming. The whole aisle was surrounded by the reflective black surfaces. She could not see in. She somehow doubted that the occupants could see out either. Upon each panel, which Nia presumed correctly to be the doors to the little pods, was another electronic screen. In white block capitals, were the names, birthdates, eye colours, hair colours, blood types and heritage of the travellers inside, with the same profiles and portraits as had been on the footman's tablet. As she walked and searched, Nia recognised some names.

Friends from school, or children from the neighbourhood. She did not like how faceless they had all become, shut off from one another behind these doors. She later presumed that it was a way of keeping the new recruits separated to avoid any kind of negativity between them – be that negativity towards one another, or negativity towards the situation. Either way, it was deathly still.

Nevertheless, she found her name. She saw her own rounded face, long blonde hair, and grey eyes glowing on the black surface, and pressed her palm against the marble-like glass. The computer calculated and read the unique patterns on her hand.

"Welcome, Ardenia Galloway," said an automated voice. "Please take your seat."

The black glass slid to one side, allowing her to walk through into the darkness within.

There really was no turning back.

SCRUTINY (N.)

Deliberate examination or observation of the actions of an individual or group. Often associated with mistrust.

I would like to pause the story for a moment to talk briefly about Nia, as well as the others we are soon to hear about:

In my notes, you can see how every being in existence has an 'electric wall of information'. An electronic fingerprint, if you will. This is their public record. Their entire existence, personality, personal preferences, and history. It includes their likes, their dislikes, their physical features, their food allergies, school grades, achievements, medical history, their fears. It is linked to the records of all their family, as well as friends and work colleagues – anyone that they are affiliated with. Any photograph, video footage, newspaper article about them that ever existed is included on this page, in this electronic file.

Due to my work, I am fortunate enough to have been granted access to all these files. I have spent years of my life dedicated to reading through each of them, aiding me in finding links between the people we discuss.

However, I have searched and searched, yet one thing remains an obstacle. A glaring, black abyss amongst the facts, truths and testimonies that are the very foundations of my research.

According to public record, Ardenia Galloway has never existed.

CHAPTER THREE

128 DAYS BEFORE

The pod was dark when she first stepped inside. It had a brilliantly clean, white leather chair, which Nia sat down in. She then watched the light from the outside corridor diminish as the door slid back into place.

It only took a few seconds before the lights turned on. It was a smooth action, which she found surprisingly calming. As was the voice which spoke to her next:

"Good morning, Nia Galloway. You prefer to be called Nia, don't you?" It was the same electronic voice that had asked her to take her seat. It was female, and very smooth. It felt as if she was speaking to Nia directly.

"This is your conductor speaking. I am delighted to see you on board with us today. I know this may all seem very strange, but you have nothing to fear. We are all here to assist you today, and over the next coming years, in becoming the greatest version of yourself. If you require assistance in any way during our journey today, please press the red button on the wall to your right. This will signal a member of the crew to your aid. Please do not leave your cabin unattended under any circumstances."

The voice, which Nia correctly presumed was pre-recorded, signalled its farewell and left her in silence. She could hear nothing going on outside her little pod, nor did she know if any of the other passengers had taken their seats around her. For some reason, she felt like it had been designed in that way for a purpose.

Oh, how little she knew.

She wondered where Jay had gotten to and how he was feeling. Nia had felt lucky to know she had a familiar face beside her on the bus. Now, however, she was just as alone as everyone else. Confined in a cupboard of blackness, with a very comfortable chair...

When she really thought about it, it wasn't all that bad. Although her head had been filled with an inexplicable doubt, she now blamed it on nothing more than an over-active process of imagination. She believed she was not in danger, that she was going to discover the best version of herself, and that the people surrounding her would be the ones to teach her how to do it. They would help her find her purpose.

> She was wrong, of course. Nia did not know that this was all planned – that this procedure had been carried out so many times that those in authority were remarkably good at predicting the behaviours and movements of their young passengers, because they believed that young passengers were incredibly predictable beings. They were not entirely wrong, I suppose. Nia, after all, had gone through the designed stages of emotion that the Authorities had expected her to: anxiety, fear, loneliness, and finally, a false sense of security. So, at that moment, whilst on a mysteriously large train, hurtling at great speeds towards an unspecified location, Nia felt reasonably satisfied.

After all, she did have a comfy chair, which was supportive in all the right places. She had privacy and a quiet space where she would not be bothered. She had a handy storage space to place her one little suitcase beside her. The temperature was nice enough and comfortable. Later, she even discovered that at the push of a button her black box of a room could reveal a window to the outside world, or display a screen on the wall in front of her on which she could read the newspaper, or request a glass of water, or watch Government documentaries. It really wasn't that bad at all...

Then there was a knock at her door: a fast, sharp knock.

"Ardenia Galloway?"

Nia was drowsy by this point, and completely unaware of how long they had been travelling for.

"Yes?"

"It is time for your medical examination."

Nia was perplexed. There had been no mention of this previously. Nia was about to ask whether she had missed an announcement, when the door suddenly slid open and a smiling lady with afro hair stood outside it. She looked awfully smart: dressed impeccably, head to toe in white, and carried a clipboard.

"Bring your things," she said. "Hurry now."

Nia was flustered. Her movements were clumsy as she followed the instruction. She followed the white-coated woman down the aisle, clutching her bag to her chest. Not a single other door was open.

"I was unaware there would be a medical examination," Nia said. She felt a trembling in her fingertips. Nia kept her head bowed low and avoided any possible chance of eye contact, not that the white-coated woman looked at her. They quick-marched down the carriages. The reassurance and comfort, as to be expected, did not come.

"Oh? No matter. We are here now. You will have a full itinerary for your next week available at your seat when you return, so there should be no more unexpected surprises."

She pressed a few buttons on a keypad on the wall. The glass doors opened to reveal a very sanitary looking corridor, with entirely grey metal walls, floors and ceilings. Nia was marched to the next set of double doors – made of metal, not glass, this time – and again, more numbers were entered into the wall before they were granted access.

The room she stood in resembled the wards she had seen at the hospital where her mother worked. Only here everything looked insanely white and somehow even more sanitised. Nia noted white partition curtains surrounding and shrouding her view of the examination tables behind, then the other young people who lay upon them. Nia felt a flutter of nervousness in her stomach. Her throat tightened. She had to remind herself once again not to be nervous. This time, her reminder had less of an effect.

She was led to the furthest bed on the left, where another female figure sat waiting for her. She, too, had a clipboard in front of her where she sat on a white stool, as well as one of the electronic screens. Nia's face was yet again glowing miserably from behind the tablet's glass.

"Ardenia, this is Doctor Suzanne Schiffer. She will be carrying out the relevant medical procedures with you today. When you are finished, I will return to escort you back to your seat."

And with that, she left the way she had come: a nameless woman, heels clicking on the hard floor as she walked away from them. Nia perched nervously on the cushioned table, facing Doctor Schiffer.

"Hello, Ardenia." She smiled, and her words were somewhat wooden. "My name is Doctor Schiffer and I will be carrying out your full medical examination today. We just want to make sure that everything is working correctly in your body, so that you have the physical capability to become your best self in name of this great country. Conducting these examinations whilst travelling will save us all time when we finally arrive at your new home."

There was a lengthy pause as Suzanne appeared to be waiting for confirmation that the woman had, indeed, vanished down the corridor. She fidgeted needlessly with the already-straight privacy curtain. Nia noticed her peeking over it discreetly until she heard the double doors sliding together once more.

Doctor Schiffer seemed to relax. Although there were other practitioners and patients behind nothing but cloth, she was clearly more at ease and more comfortable beginning her work.

"Okay, let's get started." She smiled, looking at Nia directly.

As she did so, for the first time that day Nia felt genuinely at ease in the presence of a stranger. Doctor Schiffer was not solely here to do her job. She was here to talk to her, to make sure she was okay. And Nia liked that.

"Now... Ardenia, have you had any abnormalities recently?"

"No," Nia replied.

"Any dizziness, headaches, or pain?"

"Not that I can remember, no."

"Well then, hopefully this will all just be routine."

She made innocent chit-chat to begin with. She asked Nia about her health, her life, her day. Nia watched her as she felt her stomach and tested her joints, then her reflexes and muscles. She took her heartbeat; her blood pressure; a sample of her blood. She looked in her ears, her eyes, her throat, and into her hair, at her scalp. Nia noticed as the Doctor did her work that the woman's hands were covered in very thin scars that mirrored the patterns of cracked glass: a spider's web of wounds sticking to her fingerprints and palms. When Schiffer noticed her looking at them, she rolled down her sleeves and attempted to hide the wounded skin from her.

It was when she was listening to Nia's lungs that she could not contain the question any longer. It blurted out before Nia had the chance to stop it.

"Why do you have those scars?"

It felt odd as it rolled off her tongue. It was not very often that anyone said the word 'why'. It reminded Nia of the first time she had ever called her father 'dad' instead of 'daddy'. When she first said it, it didn't feel quite right. It wasn't well practiced in her vocabulary, and she was scared it would possibly offend.

Suzanne's cold hands froze as she placed her stethoscope on Nia's back. When she spoke next, her voice was tense.

"Breathe in for me, please."

She most certainly had heard her. But there was still an exceedingly long silence before either of them said anything. Doctor Schiffer finished her examination. Then, with a tight mouth and anxious eyes, she peeked once more behind the curtain, before sitting back down opposite Nia. When she spoke, her voice was quiet, her face stern.

"It's just routine," she said quietly, "but you are not supposed to ask questions, if I'm not mistaken." Her smile had completely vanished. From her eyes, Nia could tell that her words were not borne out of anger, as she had feared they might be. More than anything else, she looked scared.

"I know," Nia said, unsure exactly what she was meant to say, "but no one has told me anything so far today. I don't know where we are going, or when I'll see the others again. This is all very confusing, and I... I just want to understand."

"That's how they rope you in," Schiffer whispered. It was barely a breath. So quiet that Nia scarcely heard the words. "They train you from the very beginning to be obedient, to blindly follow their every word... to be patient and loyal and submissive." She looked up, as if searching for some kind of help from the young girl sat in front of her, then looked down awkwardly and brushed back a single strand of hair that was out of place. She no longer looked happy and at ease, but instead appeared older than her thirty years. As if she'd seen too much of the world, as if her body and mind had been pushed to their very limits.

"I shouldn't be telling you this," she said, busying herself with papers that were already perfectly neat and filed. "You shouldn't be asking questions. Not about this."

Nia sat still, unsure of what to do. She felt like she had done something wrong, and yet Doctor Schiffer's fearful eyes were so compelling.

She shook her head, fretfully. She gripped her face in her hands and forcefully wiped a tear from her cheek with her trembling palm. "It's wrong, what they do, what they say. It's all lies. Remember that, okay? It's a trick. They don't care about you."

She stood up, her face firm again, as she finished her final medical checks on Nia. She scribbled a signature on her release form and ticked a great many boxes on the sheet of paper to confirm everything was working perfectly in the young woman's body.

"And promise me, Nia," Schiffer said, looking at Nia directly in the eyes again, "if you get even the smallest chance to run, to get out of the system, to hide from them before they start looking for you – please, *take it.*"

FABRICATE (V.)

Inventing or falsifying (something) from several components, with the intention to deceive.

Suzanne did not know that her actions here, particularly the words she spoke to Nia, would lead to her death.

Records say she was diagnosed with an unclassified mental disease called "hysteria" shortly before killing herself, just one week after meeting Ardenia Galloway on the train. I, however, disagree with the newspaper articles I have discovered during my research. I do not believe Suzanne Schiffer was the type to take her own life.

I have been to Suzanne's apartment myself. I have seen photographs after she was discovered of the room in which she supposedly hanged herself and something about the "facts" do not add up to me.

There are no beams, no doorways, no hooks to hang anything. Even the walls are bare of any form of photograph frame, or pin-up posters. There is no place for a thirty-year-old woman to hang a noose. As well as the fact that a belt was supposedly the noose of choice. But the belt presented as evidence for her suicide was of newly made leather, and too large for her own clothes, and skinny waist. It could not have belonged to her. Weak evidence. It was obvious to even the untrained eye. But scarcely any effort was made. It didn't need to be. In a world where nobody would question whether it was true or not, any form of evidence, no matter how unfitting, was enough for blind eyes to be turned.

Other evidence includes the presence of a chicken breast cooking in the oven. Carrots boiling away on the stove. I know very few people who are in the middle of preparing a meal, and suddenly get the desire to take their own life. Usually, a suicide is planned, it is strategic, it is a ceremony, of sorts. It is a final salute to a miserable existence. Suzanne would have finished cooking the meal, and she would have eaten it.

Suzanne's life was tragically taken, but it was not by her own hand.

CHAPTER FOUR

127 DAYS BEFORE

It was dark outside the window when Nia was escorted back to her seat. Needless to say, she was thoroughly confused by what had happened. The chaperone with the high-heeled shoes returned at the exact moment when Doctor Schiffer and Nia's conversation had come to an ineffable end. The doctor had handed over the release form and checked off Nia's name on her electronic tablet. The chaperone had taken the slip of paper and tucked it under the clasp of her clipboard. She briefly read through it with cold, uninterested eyes, before instructing Nia to follow her back to her designated seat.

The black door slid closed once more and Nia was in the dimly lit pod once again, alone. All she could picture was the way Doctor Schiffer had looked at her, and the spider-web scars that riddled her palms.

Nia wanted to know why she needed to run, and who she needed to run from, and to where exactly she was supposed to be running. But, of course, there was no one available to safely ask. Oh, how the questions burned in her mind. She had felt so safe just a few hours before. So happy, lazily drifting off to sleep. Could she trust the words of one strange doctor she had met on a train? In Nia's situation you can understand why she might have been hesitant.

As Nia drifted off to sleep once more, she imagined what looked like a glistening white lab coat fluttering like a flag, speckled with red flecks of paint.

In the distance, she heard a faint sound that resembled a scream, followed by the loud bang of a gunshot.

Of course, to Nia, it was all just a dream.

CHAPTER FIVE

127 DAYS BEFORE

B ella Lockett grew up on a farm. Her family lived in the same kind of house as everyone else, but theirs was next to a large, dense woodland. The farm itself was comprised of many large, tin-roofed warehouses, that were exceptionally loud inside whenever there was any rain. Here, they raised chickens for meat, which would then be sold on to shops and families across the country – all of whom appeared to be oblivious to the fact that what they were eating had once moved and clucked and scratched in the dirt. They did not see the beast. They only saw the feast. However, in a world where everyone ate the same thing, chicken seemed a logical feast due to how quickly they could be bred.

Bella was the first in her small family to go to Camp Clandestine for nearly thirty years. Due to both her parents being without siblings - her grandparents long dead - and her younger brother being only just old enough to walk on his own feet, Bella was very much without company on her journey at the beginning of Autumn that year.

This was not unfamiliar, of course. Many children were not as lucky as Ardenia Galloway to have someone in their family of similar age to them. However, most others knew at least someone. A friend from school, perhaps. Bella did not have anybody. When she set off that September morning, she was completely alone.

She was not the most likeable of children, even when she

was small. Her father's grizzly job and her mother's encouraging yet fierce upbringing (and aggressive enthusiasm) led Bella to be a rather bossy child. She was blunt, and not especially feminine in her words. This abrasive exterior meant she really did not care that she had no one to sit next to at school. Bella was a very rare breed of child, who very much enjoyed being alone.

She was not dependent on people. She was not dependent on money. She was not dependent on the innocence and joy that life brings. She was not dependent on the opinions of others. She was quite happy with what she had, if not less, and preferred to use her time alone pondering the workings of the world.

This was what made her a threat.

More than once, there had been an ominous knock at the front door of their countryside house, with an Authority stood waiting on the porch steps. Bella remembered being only a small child and peering up at the man with the dark, slicked-back hair and the black suit, and the black hat, glaring at her with his black eyes. He had threatened her father to keep Bella under control. Bella was asking too many questions. Bella was a child who may not live to see her Graduation Day.

And so, she had been hushed by her parents, and kept away from the others, and been made even more solitary than she already was. She had been told not to speak while at school and to never ask a question again – not outside of the house – or she would be taken away.

"To where?" she had asked.

"To your death, dear one."

You would think an answer so blunt and foreboding would frighten a child.

Not Bella.

It was at age six that Bella Lockett decided to uncover the lies that blanketed the eyes of the world. Even if it meant she ran the risk of being taken away.

CHAPTER SIX

126 DAYS BEFORE

I t was Bella Lockett who approached Nia Galloway on that first day at Camp Clandestine, amongst the hustle and the bustle of the crowds.

Nia did not feel the train stop, but as it did so an announcement was made through the overhead speakers. It roused her gently from her sleep. The same pre-recorded, sickly-honey-sweet female voice wafted over the airwaves once more.

She exited her seat when the black door slid noiselessly open, to see every other person doing the same. They all formed a perfectly straight line throughout the aisle of the carriage, without having to try. There was a lot of looking about between them, as they searched in one another's faces for a sense of meaning and direction. Nia searched in the crowd for Jay, but she could not see him. All the passengers in Nia's carriage were of the same status as her – female.

The line shuffled forward, one equidistant step at a time. As they got off, their identities were checked again, and their faces matched against their photographs; horrific as they still were, shining brightly on a glass sheet of paper.

Their destination was a huge, perfectly square building, that was once white, but had since been aged and dirtied with pollution from the air, turning it a foul desaturated grey. Again, like the train, and like the platform, it appeared to stretch for countless miles in both directions. From each carriage, the orderly lines were steadily converging into fewer, longer ones, in order to get through one of the entrances. There were countless barriers lined end to end along only a small portion of the entrance. Fifty, at a guess, possibly more, and each was disconcertingly busy. If you have ever been to a busy underground station and watched as the many travellers try to get through those barriers with their tickets as quickly and efficiently as they can manage, the scene echoed such organised chaos. Crowded, confusing, but steadily easing into a quiet order, with time.

That is when Bella Locket made her entrance.

Nia felt a shove from behind her, which sent her toppling to the floor. Legs and identical shoes surrounded her at eye level. She tried to stand, only to find a hand holding her down for a moment longer.

"Terribly sorry," the female voice said.

A hand grabbed hold of Nia's, one that didn't feel quite right. Bella was holding a piece of paper in her palm, which she placed in the centre of Nia's hand before letting go.

"Here's your bag," the girl said. "I'm Bella."

"Nia."

"I know who you are." Bella smiled. Her bright green eyes sparkled. "I read about your father, Paul Galloway, in the newspaper. He was Curious, wasn't he?"

Nia's heart almost stopped when she heard that word. It was barely a whisper, and she knew no one else would have heard, but she still looked around herself to the other lines of people to see if anyone was looking at her.

Bella's words, despite Nia's denial, had shook her to the core. Her father had recently disappeared for a short time and returned nothing more than the shell of the man he used to be. Not even Nia knew what had happened to him for certain, it had been too well covered up by the Authorities. She had hoped that no one else had heard of it either.

And yet this red-haired, bright-eyed stranger that stood before her seemed to know the hidden truths of her family, despite never having seen her before.

> Curiousness was a so-called disease that people were taught to fear. It was supposedly a virus that was so strictly prohibited for fear of contagion that there were strict regulations for it. It was taught to be so fast-spreading and deadly that anyone caught with it was taken away and put into solitary confinement until they recovered, and a fair few were never seen again.

> This was all bullshit, of course. Curiousness is a state of mind, not a physical disease, and it would pose no threat to being physically contagious in the way that a disease such as the flu or the measles is. It was merely a form of propaganda; a way to stop the population questioning their own lives, and the way the country was run. It was a way to stop any ideas of revolution and change spreading, and the idea of free-will returning.

Nia looked down at the piece of paper that was now screwed up in her own palm. With shaking fingers, and being very conscious of the people surrounding her, she opened it as discreetly as she could, and looked down...

FREEDOM OF THOUGHT. FREEDOM OF LIFE. FREEDOM
OF EXPRESSION. DOWN WITH THE OPPRESSION.
LONG LIVE THE REVOLUTION.
Catch hold of me again if you want to join the fight.

Nia's throat closed. She tightened her fist around the paper, and she shoved it deep inside her coat pocket. This was treason. A bold, forbidden, illegal act.

This was the moment that Ardenia Galloway learned of the revolution, and when she learned that a single spark in a dry grass field can cause the whole world, as we know it, to burn.

TACITURN (ADJ.)

Referring to an individual who is quiet or uncommunicative with speech.

Nia's response to this name-calling was not, as you may presume, an overreaction.

It was seen not as a crime, but almost a sin. A dirty hateful thing to be and to do. Even the subtlest trace of Curiousness was enough to have someone blacklisted for the rest of their days on their Government record.

Nia's father had such a mark. Nobody in the family, not even their mother, knew the story of why Paul Galloway had been taken away in the middle of the night by three men dressed in black, or why he had not come home for some weeks. It was possible that it had been entirely fabricated for propaganda means – as a simple deterrent for all those in the area to remain with their mouths shut and their heads down.

Not much was known about the rules behind Curiousness. I, too, have failed to discover an actual written law that says it was a crime. It was more an unspoken rule, a societal norm, to simply continue in life with a stiff upper lip. To take your share, and then to be on your way before it was taken from you.

The rules for children were slightly different, due to Curiousness in children being innate and somewhat required for their basic learning of skills. You see, being Curious was a label not for those who asked any old questions, but to those who asked the wrong questions.

Those who questioned their way of life, their existence, the way things were run – those who posed a threat to the Dictator.

Nia's father, to say the least, was not the same man when he returned home from his 'quarantine'.

His arm had been tattooed with the trademark word across

both of his wrists, underneath which was the Dictator's symbol, and he now had a deep scar running the length of his neck. Inside, they were warned, under the skin, just about visible, was a large wire that was connected to his heart and held a microphone at the opposite end. If Mister Galloway was heard to be speaking or asking questions about anything he should not, they did not know what would happen to him. But the ferocity and adamant ways in which his feeble self now acted were difficult to watch. The man trembled with fright when anyone so much as made a suggestion towards him.

Of course, the effects wore down, as no man can keep up such a heightened level of anxiety up for any length of time. But he was never quite the same man he had used to be.

He no longer drank, nor engaged in group conversation. He became increasingly quiet and withdrawn – a mere expressionless observer who lived only to listen, and to serve. He became so abundantly submissive to any Authority and worked harder than he ever had done in his life. But the wire was never removed. Nia grew up with a different father to the one who had held her tenderly in his arms when she was born.

It was a sad situation, but the human spirit has an unwavering ability to persevere, to make do and to survive. It is a trait that some might call a blessing. To others, it is nothing more than a wretched curse that forced them to continue clawing themselves through each day, in the mechanical, boring world of slavery in which they lived.

CHAPTER SEVEN

126 DAYS BEFORE

E ddie Johnson was a member of the armed forces. He had joined as soon as he was able, completing his training early at Camp Clandestine to serve for his country. It was his family honour – his duty as a member of the Johnson family. It was a tradition within the male lineage. He was born a Johnson, and he would die a Johnson. Fighting for his family, for his Government and for the future of others on the battleground.

At age sixteen, the tale he had been told painted a somewhat bleak and predictable picture for his future. The age of which men and women could join the army of their own accord was getting lower and lower with every generation. Due to his father's high status, he had been granted exclusive access through the education system earlier than others. Eddie was the first of the Johnson line who had been too young to start a family before he was signed up. His father had ensured he completed his lieutenant training alongside his Third Year mandatory education. At twenty one, Eddie was the first liutenant in history to be below the age of twenty five.

The first-born son. It was written. And, it must be said, there may have been some genetic predisposition for impeccable service in the armed forces, as Eddie was an incredibly respected man. The years he had spent so far in service had made his father proud. He had learned a great deal and was now a teacher of new recruits at Camp Clandestine. He instructed recruits through their physical training. This was his first year on such a duty. He believed it was going reasonably well.

That was, until he had seen the exchange occur outside the barriers of the front gate on the very first day.

The new recruits moved forward through the crowd. There was no shoving, of course, but people were far closer to one another than Eddie presumed they would have liked to be. Eddie stood by one of the many electronically controlled barriers, which checked the identity of each of the passers-by. It was steadily filtering the rabble into neat rows before they passed through the gates. By each electronic barrier, as it scanned the fingerprints and took pictures of each timid face, a guard stood, just like Eddie. They were all silently wielding an arm-length gun, which, if you can imagine it, was a rather menacing sight – enough to make your butt-cheeks tense, just a little. They were instructed to stand, entirely motionless, and to intervene and report anything that was not part of the structured plan of initiation. The suits they wore were of black weather-proof material, covered in black plates of light-weight armour which were resistant to pretty much everything, or so it was said. They weighed nothing but deflected everything. A black reflective visor covered their eyes for shielding away the sun, and for protecting their own identity. They had been trained to look like statues. Dark, menacing statues.

It was on this day, by his gate, that Eddie had seen it. He watched, from behind his visor, two female figures in the crowd. Both pale, both out of place. A girl with blonde hair was bumped into by one with curly ginger locks. There had been a scuffling, some awkwardness, and the exchange of a note. The blonde girl had then somehow turned even paler, stuffing the note deep into her pocket with a hurried motion. It was as if she thought it would screech of its own accord if left out in the open.

Nia was trying her best to blend in, and the note, where it bulged in her pocket, felt like it was burning against her hip, threatening to get out. Her woollen coat would do her no good if her fear-stricken face was giving the game away. She focused on looking as submissive as she possibly could. She had looked into the vacant eyes of her father so many times, it was as if she were staring into nothing more than a lifelike mirror. Then she stepped forth towards the barriers with an expression which she hoped was nothing more than a reflection of her father's feeble form.

Eddie watched the scene unfurl before him. He was well aware of what had transpired. He knew as well as anyone: it was his duty. He must retrieve that note from the girl. All his training from his seniors, the Government, the drills, had hammered into him that any suspicious activity must be sought out and snuffed out, as soon as possible. Any hint, any possible spark, any flicker of Curiousness must be extinguished before the ideas were ablaze in the heads of many. The Curious – the diseased, as they were sometimes called – were quarantined to stop the virus spreading. He had never before had to execute someone himself.

The girl approached. Eddie thrust his arm out, blocking her way. Her eyes were so wide it was as if they were screaming at him. So wide, he could see his own reflection.

He had reached out to stop her, to pull her aside, but he saw in her face how terrified she was – and how faceless he had become. He saw his reflection, emotionless and unblinking, staring back at him. He'd finally been confronted with the mirror image of the machine that he'd been manipulated into – and it was an image that burned in his mind and shocked him to his core: a whirring cog in a destructive machine.

He saw innocence in her young face, despite the spark in her pocket. The rigidity of his exterior relaxed, his arm lowered.

He let her pass through.

The girl stood for her photograph and waited for it to be cross-referenced with her records. Her fingerprints were scanned. The light glowed green, allowing her through. She let go the breath she had been holding in her chest.

Eddie blinked, unsure of himself, unsure of the extent of the damage he may or may not be guilty of playing a part in.

He had surprised himself that day. He had taken a step back and looked properly at himself through the eyes of another. He knew there was little more he could do now, but he was somewhat anxious to see how things panned out, and to see the girl again.

Opposite him, across the crowds, he watched the final young people step off the train. The carriage doors closed, and it set off in the direction that it had come.

The only exit from Camp Clandestine had gone. There was no way for any of them to return home.

PROPAGANDA (N.)

Information and materials, most notably of a biased nature, used to evoke support for political views or causes.

Clandestine is a word which is now used today to describe something which is secret or forbidden, usually due to the fact that the action in question is considered unlawful. The Camp that Nia had been sent to in the last days of her youth was named not due to it being illegitimate, but due to the man who it had been named after. Major Michelangelo Clandestine was a man who had been favoured by the Dictator for some many years and had shown explicit dedication and loyalty to the Government. He was a military officer, who had designed the programme for each of the new cadets to follow to ensure they became the greatest version of themselves and could give to the country the best they had to offer. He had dark swept-back hair, a swarthy stubbly beard and rugged appearance. He always wore a freshly pressed suit and designer wristwatches, which he just could not flaunt enough.

The training that each individual must go through at The Camps, as designed by Clandestine, was advertised as being a life-changing experience for all – one where every young person discovers who they are and what their place is within the country. Posters, television reels, banners and announcements all glorified these three years as the making of each man and woman.

As with any propaganda, the reality was very different.

Nia was one of many that day who had her details confirmed, and her individuality withdrawn. It was the day she would begin to realise that being Ardenia Galloway meant nothing, and that she would only ever be worthy of anyone's affections when she made a grand yet faceless contribution to the economy.

Michelangelo Clandestine had designed it this way so that all those below him would never get the appreciation they deserved for their actions. He designed it so they always felt like they just weren't good enough, and he took credit for more ideas (that were not his own) than I would care to admit. He was charming, dashing, arrogant and cruel - and was in marvellously close companionship with the Dictator. Their friendship was a rigorously shaken shitstorm of a cocktail, as dangerous as you can get.

You must admit though, that the dramatic irony of his name is something remarkable to behold.

CHAPTER EIGHT

126 DAYS BEFORE

Nia sat in a large auditorium with a glass dome roof. Surrounding her sat every other cadet that had travelled that day on the train. The room had wooden pews for seats. They had been polished so expertly that Nia found herself slipping about slightly as she sat down.

She was sat some levels up – easily four stories high. She couldn't count the number of heads below her, all waiting in anticipation like herself. Nobody else had taken off their coats or hats. Nia decided it was best if she left hers on, too.

"Ladies, Gentlemen – children of the *future*!"

The introduction startled Nia slightly. A man with a polished suit and equally polished smile walked out onto the stage below. His suit was blue pinstriped, his hair dark and swept back. An angular, meticulously groomed beard decorated his cheeks and chin.

"We are ever so delighted to have you all here today - all of you excited, no doubt. All with young minds waiting to be *moulded.*"

Somebody sneezed, a few levels below. Nia couldn't see who it was. For some reason, she had a feeling that the culprit had vibrant red hair. The crumpled note in Nia's pocket seemed to burn against her skin.

The man continued. "Before you begin this incredible educational journey, I wanted to introduce myself. I am Michelangelo, and unfortunately today may be the only day you see me here at Camp Clandestine. You see, I am a *very* busy man and in great demand, all over the country. As Head of Education, and with close connection to the Dictator, I am afraid I do not have the time to get to know you all on a *personal* level... "

Michelangelo, Head of Education, paused. He winked at somebody in the front row. Nia felt her face grimace, but quickly tried to correct it, in case somebody noticed.

" ...but here I am, today, just for you. I see your shiny, happy, eager faces staring back at me and I just *know* that the future of the Dictator, *and* this great country, are in trusting hands!" He clasped his palms together and beamed like a proud, if slightly creepy, father. "I am *so* delighted to welcome you here today, and to get to see you all before the magic happens. And with that, shall we see what is in store for you all in the next three years?"

If Michelangelo was awaiting a response, he did not get it. The crowd stayed deathly still. You could have heard a pin drop in that room. Regardless, Michelangelo appeared unphased. He clapped his hands together twice, and a gleaming silver screen began to descend from the ceiling.

"Lights, please!"

The room was quickly plunged into darkness. A vibrant beam of white light lit up the silver screen. Across it read the words:

CADET CAMP INTRODUCTORY VIDEO 1

The video was filmed in black and white – presumably the original video from when the Camps had first opened, some generations ago. It opened to display several rows of marching soldiers, all stepping in unison. It was a clip that Nia had seen several times over on the television set back at home.

> The video reeled on. It spoke of how noble it was for all the cadets to be there that day – not that any of them had a choice

in the matter. It spoke of how a lot of cadets presumed that the Camps are not a nice place to be – and how wrong that presumption was (apparently).

The video talked of the great many things that the Camps could offer the young students – a thriving social life, wonderful exercise regimes, the chance to recognise the great potential that lay within themselves. It promised the cadets that they would, undoubtedly, love it here. They would become everything that they had always wanted to be – and more. They would serve their country, they would prepare for war, they would live to fulfil the Dictator's demands, and they would do so willingly. They would stamp out Curiousness, they would be given their future employment roles. They would go through the fool-proof marital partner match-making systems and be given their ideal mate. There really was nothing bad that could come out of their time here at Camp Clandestine. It would be hard work, but every ounce of effort would be rewarded tenfold. The future of the country would depend on those cadets. And the cadets would do their families, their country, and their Dictator, proud.

Now, I've watched this video, and I have to say, they did a good job. It really does look like they're inviting you to live at Disneyland, free of charge. But with the knowledge I have now, looking back on what they managed to get away with... it's baffling. I can't believe they managed to blatantly lie like that and just got away with it. I don't know about you, but it makes me want to vomit, just a little bit.

Michelangelo stepped back onto the stage as the lights turned on once more.

"How about that then, folks?" He was certainly excited, and his polished grin stretched even further across his face.

Nia felt the note in her pocket and went to touch it with her fingers – but caught herself, just in time. She didn't want to draw any attention to it. The results could be disastrous. All she wanted was to get out of that room, filled with hundreds of people, and find a way to dispose of it.

"I must dash off and leave you now, younglings. But as sad as I am that I have to go, I will leave you with this: everything you do here at Camp Clandestine will be watched, will be monitored, will be tested. Our camps have the highest success rates in the entire world – only the greatest of all students pass through our gates and pass our tests. You have the capability to be one of those students. I believe in you. Good luck."

He went to leave, but then stopped, caught himself, and added: "Oh, and don't forget to smile, pretty ones" – he pointed up to the corner of the room, where a blinking eye was perched – "you're on camera!"

The room Nia stood in was cold and almost entirely grey. Every bare brick, every floorboard, every thread in every piece of cloth seemed to look tired and worn...lifeless.

I have been to this room myself. I have seen the spacious dorms that each cadet was given – now entirely out of use, of course, and nothing but a tragic memory. They were entirely abandoned and still fully furnished, even if the only occupants there now are rats, insects, and the occasional bird. The glass windows were broken when I visited Nia's room, and the curtains flapped about in the ceaseless wind. But I couldn't help but think when I was there that it was as if the soul had been sucked from the room itself. A black hole steadily emptying the furnishings and all who touched them, with every passing second. The rooms originally were probably not so aged, or outdated, or as grey as I have seen them – but I cannot imagine, through all their years of use, that they were much happier places to live. They did not live up to the advertisements, that was for sure. They did not reflect the gleaming, warm photographs of smiling cadets surrounded by friends, in lavish, homely rooms – and they most certainly were not places filled with love. They did not appear to fulfil every need for home comforts, nor echo the warm sense of satisfaction that comes from curling up in your own bed at your parents' house. They were cold. They were hollow.

On the wall to the right as she entered the room, Nia saw a large, horrific-looking clock. The second hand loudly *tick-tick-ticked* from ceiling to floor, round and round it went. Across the face of the clock read the words 'Time Spent in Servitude Will Make a Man Rich.' Nia noticed how it did not specify which man.

The tired floorboards groaned as she walked across them towards the bed and set her single bag down onto the mattress. She set herself down, too, and the bedsprings spoke back to the floorboards in a similar tone.

It was quiet. So very quiet. As if the building and everyone in it were holding their breath in anticipation.

Nia was certainly in that description.

Through her coat pocket, she could feel the soft edges of the crumpled note. It felt so much bigger than it really was, resting against her hip, due to the large burden that it carried with it. It felt as large to her as the lump in her throat.

She opened her suitcase and hung her clothes in the squeaky wardrobe. She ran her fingers along the edge of the wood, searching furtively for wires, cameras, microphones, speakers – anything that did not belong. She took her toothbrush and bar of soap into the tiny bathroom – an unexpected privilege – and searched the sink, the light, the fan, the mirror.

Nothing to be found. There was nothing behind the mirror at all, much to her surprise. She took her notebook, her pen and her writing papers and set them down on the small wooden desk next to the window. In the drawers – nothing. Under the seat – nothing. Behind the desk itself... nothing.

Nia steadily began to relax. With her few possessions now in their new homes, she reached again into her pocket to feel for the note, while she searched the remainder of the room with her eyes for anywhere a camera could be watching.

The clock on the wall, which must have been six feet in diameter, *tick-tick-tick*ed away. From where she sat on the bed, her eyes followed the huge second hand around and around, until...

Her breath caught.

She diverted her gaze straight down and busied herself with putting away her little suitcase under the bed. It took longer than probably necessary.

There, in the centre of the clock, where each of the three hands met, was the tiny blinking eye of a camera.

She was not so alone, after all.

Breathing slowly, she stood up once more, and turned to face the window. In what she hoped was a seamless, unnoticeable movement, she grabbed the note from her pocket, then used the same hand to open the window –

CLANG

The noise made her jump, and her gaze rose sharply in alarm. The nerves had made her blind to the thin iron bars that covered the outside of the windowpane like a small cage. The window frame colliding with them in her haste to discard the note.

She took a breath to compose herself and, being very mindful of the watchful eye of the clock bearing into her back, she pushed her hand through the small gap in the window and against the bars. The spaces in between each one were not enough to get her knuckles past, but she squeezed her fingertips together and found she could stretch through a few more inches.

As soon as her fist was as far out into the open as it could physically go, she dropped the note and watched it flutter away in the wind.

She watched. She waited. Her heart thumped harder than ever against her chest. She thought of the microphone implanted into her father's neck and shuddered, praying that the same fate did not lie in store for her. Her hand grasped at her own neck instinctively.

Knock-knock-knock.

Her whole body stiffened.

Knock-knock-knock.

Someone was at her door.

OPPRESSED (ADJ.)

Subject to hardship and harsh treatment, most notably by the unjust hand of a member of authority.

My research of Nia's personal experience is only so well documented due to the fact that Nia wrote a diary during her time as a member of the revolution. You may be wondering how Nia managed to write a diary in a society that was so oppressed and filled with surveillance.

She was a smart girl – much smarter and much more aware than many people gave her credit for.

Her mind worked differently to the rest – even if she did not know it yet.

CHAPTER NINE

126 DAYS BEFORE

K *nock-knock-knock.*
There it was again. The third time. Nia had to answer it. If she didn't, it would only raise further suspicion.

They saw it.

They must have done.

She straightened her coat and brushed down the now-empty pocket. She felt as exposed and terrified as one might do if they climb the stairs in the dark and plunge their foot into nothingness upon reaching the top.

She pulled her hair back and pushed it behind her shoulders.

Deep breath, small smile for the cameras, GO.

The floorboards creaked. Her knees wobbled. She reached out and unlocked the door, ready to see armed officers, ready to be taken away, ready to vanish, to be deleted from every record, every archive – to have her entire existence erased.

She opened the door.

"Jay!"

She fell into his arms, and was reminded of earlier that morning when they had clung to one another in fear. It was almost the same moment, yet everything felt so utterly different.

"Don't come in," she said, perhaps too sharply, when he made to step over the threshold.

"Why?"

"There's a camera. If you're here, they can't see you."

"Nia, are you–?"

"I'm sure. In the clock, on the wall. They're watching all of us."

Jay stepped backwards slightly. "Nia, you're scaring me. Is everything okay?"

"Yes." She shifted uncomfortably. "Something came up, but I dealt with it. I'm just glad you're alright."

They smiled at each other. The corridor felt so quiet. Jay's voice was hushed as his fingers fidgeted on the wooden door-frame.

"Same to you. I don't think we'll get to see each other much while we're here. Something tells me they'll frown on people talking. Did you see how they separated us all on the train?"

"Yes, I think I agree. That's probably why they've given us all separate rooms too... How'd you find me?"

"There is a list at the end of each corridor of who's in each room."

"Why?"

"I don't know. It's strange for it to be out in the open. Usually any kind of document they have is so hidden. But there must be a reason for it."

"Maybe it's so we know who our enemies are," Nia suggested. It was a poor attempt at humour.

"Or our competitors," Jay said. "One of the guys said that people's names get scratched off each week if they don't make it to the next stage of testing."

There was a long moment as each of them looked at each other and their smiles faded into nothing. They realised just how sinister the rumour sounded, and how true it might just be.

"Jay, I'm scared," Nia said. She gripped the door until her knuckles were white.

"I am too." He looked down. "Do you think we'll make it back home?"

Nia saw how he was searching for hope, not the truth. But she saw no point in hiding from it when their fate began the very next day.

"No," she answered. "That's for certain. Whoever we are today won't be the people who head back to mum and dad's house. If we go back at all."

Jay nodded slowly. The grimness of the situation seemed to grip him in that moment. He looked like he was about to be sick.

"On the train... " Nia said, "I was given a medical examination by a woman called Suzanne Schiffer. She had been to the camp before."

"What'd she say?"

"Not much. Not much at all really, about what happened. But she was afraid. She was really shaken by whatever she'd experienced here. And her hands were covered in scars, like broken glass. She told me that if I get the chance, I should run away from this place, and never look back."

"Why are you telling me this, Nia?"

"I don't know. I felt like it was... important somehow."

"I think it's important too," he said, "but I also think it is too much to think about now – and too risky to talk about in an open corridor."

"I agree," Nia said. "Tomorrow's when our lives begin, or so I am told."

Jay gave a quick nod. "Good luck."

"Same to you."

They shared a long, fearful look, before Jay turned to go and Nia closed the door.

The empty room stared back at her. Even with the blinking eye of the camera staring from the clock, and the knowledge that there were others just like her all around, she had never, ever, felt so alone.

CHAPTER TEN

125 DAYS BEFORE

Nia awoke the next morning to the clock chiming six. Curled beneath the bedsheets, covered by her nightie and blanket, she wiped the grit from her eyes. She had hardly slept that night at all. She had been terrified by the knowledge that she was forever being watched and was more separate from the world than she had ever been before. It had all been too much when she had been alone in the darkness, and sleep eluded her.

But this was her first day. This was the beginning of a new Nia, apparently.

The clock face watched her as she washed and dressed. Its words would be soon imprinted on the inside of her eyelids, as they were when she left the room that morning.

Time spent in servitude will make a man rich.

As she closed and locked the door behind her, she found herself questioning – *why a man, and not a woman?*

CHAPTER ELEVEN

125 DAYS BEFORE

Eddie awoke at 05:00, just as the sun was beginning to peek through the darkness and into the day. His mornings were all the same routine as they had been since he was sixteen.

He awoke. He stretched. He brushed his teeth. He changed. He did press-ups, sit-ups, chin-ups, bench-presses. He ran. He ran around the entire perimeter of the camp. He showered, he changed again. He combed back his hair. He put on his tags, as he stared at his reflection. He wondered if the day would be entirely different to the days he had lived before.

Usually, the answer was no.

On this day, the answer was different.

The air was chilly. Not surprising for a morning in early Autumn. The walk to the Assembly Room appeared shorter than previous trips. His thoughts eluded him that day. His brain was dull and empty from the routine.

The day ran as it normally did. When Eddie entered the room, he was struck with the abnormally cold temperature. The entirely white, metal furniture seemed to suck any remaining warmth away from anyone who entered. It was colder inside than it was out. This was how the Authorities liked it. They did not want the students to feel too comfortable in their surroundings. Eddie walked to the front of the room. The sound of his polished boots were the only sound in the otherwise silent hall. Rows of empty chairs stared back at him. He obtained his position at the front, dead centre, stood straight.

Good posture is self-respect, his father always said.

The clock on the opposite wall read 07:21. In exactly nine minutes, the room would be filled by exactly one hundred people. Fifty males, fifty females. They would sit on respective sides of the room, an information pack in their laps. Eddie would talk for fifteen minutes and give the same speech he gave to every Induction Class, as he had done for for the past year as a training Lieutenant for Camp Clandestine. This was his first year as fully qualified and unsupervised in the position. He would give his speech many times in the following day, until every new cadet had been thoroughly introduced to the future that awaited them.

The clock struck 07:28, and two lines marched into the room. They filled each seat systematically. Eddie stood perfectly still and watched the second hand of the clock tick around its face. At 07:29 the room was exactly half full. At 07:30, everyone was seated and instantly settled, under the watchful eyes of the escorts who stood at the end of each room. They were dressed entirely in white from head to toe, their hair pulled back and their cotton tunics impeccably ironed. Their faces, Eddie noticed, were completely emotionless – entirely empty. He could not tell if they were bored people, or if they were even people at all.

He took a breath, and began:

"Ladies, gentlemen, the makers of the future. Today is the day when the rest of your life begin, and you can finally contribute to this great country and make your elders proud to call you their equals. Your country needs you, more than you ever thought imaginable, and today is the start of your opportunity to become great... to become knowledgeable... to become strong.

"As you can see from the folders in front of you, there is an extensive training programme lined up for you. This has been tailored and shaped over many years to ensure that the best is brought forth from all of you. The capability for greatness lies within you, and over the next three years we aim to shape you into the people you were born to be – servants of the country, like all of us here already.

"There will be opportunities for you on several occasions to display to your elders exactly what you are made of. A prime of example of this is Elimination Day. This elite test of physical and mental capabilities will differentiate the most prestigious from the rest. If you are chosen to be put forward for this test, you have the opportunity to earn the title of Supreme Cadet. This is not an easy title to gain, and it comes with a great many privileges. I was awarded as Supreme Cadet all three years of my training here. That is how I stand before you as a lieutenant now. I strongly suggest you try your hardest from your first day here. It is the only way you will be able to pass the tests that await you.

"You will learn further education in an area of your choosing, as well as detailed history of our country, and the expectation held of you for the future. You will also undergo an intensive fitness training course and learn how to fight in combat. There is a great war to soon be upon us from the West, from a country far across the sea. We must be ready for it. And you must be ready, like all of us here, to defend your country, and its ruler – the great and noble Dictator."

"This course is not optional. Every single one of you here will pass and will leave with a certification that is the same as everyone else's. You will not have the option to fail."

He gave a stern, thoughtful look to the crowd and surveyed their faces. Peaky and somewhat petrified. This was how he had been told they should look. He noticed the wide and fearful eyes of the blonde he had seen the previous afternoon. Her pale lips were a taught, timid line, and her blonde hair was pulled back neatly into an efficient plait. When he caught her gaze, she looked down almost immediately.

"My name is Lieutenant Johnson. I will be leading and assisting some of the training sessions for some of you here. You will not address me nor anyone else of authority by their first name at these camps. You will not call me mister. You will not call me Johnson. You will call me either Sir, or Lieutenant."

He witnessed a few of them gulp and sighed internally to himself. Eddie did not particularly enjoy intimidating those who were already intimidated. he realised it would be a tough job to get used to. He took a breath:

"Everything you will experience in the next month has been highly detailed in the folders you hold. Those folders are for you to take back to your dorm rooms and read in your own time. Almost any question you could possibly want to ask, the answer can be found in there. However, if it is not, you can find my details in there too. But I warn you – do not waste my time.

"Your orientation today will consist of a tour of the premises, an overview of your assessments, and expectations for the first six months, lunch, and the opportunity to socialise with your fellow cadets to become part of a working team.

"Full training begins tomorrow at 0800 hours. Do not be late. Refer to your folder for your timetable. Does anyone have any questions for me now, or would like me to repeat myself?"

Eddie was met with stunned silence. No one dared move, least of all raise their hand. All eyes avoided his own.

"Right then. With that, good luck on your course. Work hard, follow the rules, and follow the crowd. I'll see you tomorrow."

He stood felt an empty sense of pride at being able to regurgitate once more the memorised speech his father had dictated to him. Row by row the room emptied, just as his heart did with every group he had to terrify.

He sighed, his hands behind his back as he stood up straight. Conditioning had a deadly way of sneaking into the unconscious mind.

He saw the blonde girl exit and found himself wishing she would look his way. Another beautiful woman his father would forbid him to touch without permission.

"*We take advantage of only a select few,*" he always said, "*the rest live to willingly serve us."*

But Eddie did not wish to be served, nor did he wish to take advantage of another. He wished for something real, he wished to love. And in his heart he knew that serving and loving were two very different things.

He lived to serve his country – but he would not die loving it.

GREED (N.)

Intense and unsettling desire for something, most often wealth, food, or power. Associated with selfishness.

Eddie Johnson's father was not a good man.

Edward Johnson Sr. was a Colonel in the armed forces and was a well-respected man. He had certainly embraced a life in service, since he was a young boy, and was living his dream each day when he got to bark orders at people, and have others fetch him things.

People like Edward Johnson were one of the many problems that was faced back then, back when the world was falling apart. It was women and men like him who we might say had a substantial influence on nationwide affairs, and who only added to the problem.

Have you ever met a man who is instantly dislikeable? He doesn't even have to open his mouth, but you can tell somehow from the way he dresses, the way he does his hair, or, more notably, that smug countenance on his face? You can tell as soon as he enters the room that, in his head, he owns everyone and everything, and he likes it that way. He will argue with anyone about anything until both are blue in the face, because he feels like he's already won, and he'll never accept the opinion of the other. Because that would be admitting defeat, and would make a dent in his huge, inflated head.

Edward Johnson Sr. had such an inflated ego that I am genuinely surprised he could fit through his own front door (and he had a very large house, with a very large front door, might I add). How he survived in the army as long as he did, with such a large target balanced between his shoulders, I will never know.

He awoke in the morning in a miraculously comfortable

bed, after a night's sleep that the humble folk can only dream of (oh, what irony). He spent his entire day bossing people about, taking advantage of others, selfishly taking everything he possibly could for himself, and surrounding himself with brown-nosed ass-kissers who told him how great he was in the hopes he would fork out a handful of his blessings to another.

He never did.

This is the kind of person who led the world to shit, so many years ago.

Selfish, greedy – would not hesitate to throw someone else in harm's way if it meant he could have more of things he already had too much of.

Those kinds of people just don't know how to make do – they don't know how to be happy.

They don't know when to stop.

CHAPTER TWELVE

124 DAYS BEFORE

The first day had arrived for Nia. Her morning was slightly different to Eddie's. The campus was large and buzzing with activity. Nia decided quite shortly after seeing it that morning that she did not like it.

All were awoken sharply at 06:00 with the giant wall clock chiming its malicious, monotonous tone for the longest minute of Nia's short life so far. It was old, and it was shrill. Having slept very little, she was already mostly awake. She did not like the noise, she did not like her bed, and she did not like it here.

Regardless, she got up, and changed into the uniform that hung in her wardrobe.

Although the uniform fit her perfectly around the curves of her body, she did not quite feel comfortable, nor like herself. The flag of the country and the names of the Government were emblazoned across her chest and arm, alongside the Dictator's flag. The fabric felt full of starch, and was itchy around her neck. Her name and her personalised identification number were embroidered onto both the front and the back of her torso, and yet the clothes she wore could not feel less like her own.

She straightened her green blazer, smoothed her matching skirt, tightened her grey tie, fixed her hair and slipped into her stockings and shoes.

Something just didn't feel right about it to her. It was her duty to her country, her right as a citizen, her obligation as a young person, like all the advertisement slogans had said. She was no different to anyone else.

Regardless, she stayed put, as if she had entered a room and forgotten why she had chosen to go in there in the first place.

Had she chosen?

It was too late to ponder. The clock face read 06:30. She took a deep breath and braced herself for the day ahead.

The first day of her future.

The canteen was on the ground floor of her dorm block. Nia followed others silently down polished metal steps, hearing nothing but the tapping of shoes on each stair.

They made no conversation. They merely followed their growling stomachs and the smells of cooked sausages and buttered toast downwards until they reached the bottom. It smelled like good, hearty food. And why wouldn't it be? An army needs to be strong. To be strong, it needs to be fuelled. They were feeding them up.

Queueing up with a plastic tray reminded Nia of school. She was not given a choice. You ate what they gave you, and they gave everyone the same. The faces of the catering staff looking just as unamused and lifeless as every other worker Nia had ever come across.

While she waited in line to be served her helpings, Nia's eyes glimpsed the flaming curls. The girl's green eyes seemed to flash when she saw Nia, and she gave a smile that looked warm and kind, and so genuinely happy and pleased to see her – it was a smile that made Nia look away, sharply, as if just a glance in her direction burned her corneas.

She hurriedly took her tray of sausages, beans, scrambled eggs and toast, and found a spare seat at a table which was far away from the girl. The other students looked up at her with their anxious faces for a moment as she sat down, then went back to pushing the food around their trays. There was certainly a tension in the air. It was a tenseness that was highly contagious and all-consuming, one which Nia begged to be broken. She was suddenly no longer hungry.

Her mother had raised her to always attempt to eat something at mealtimes, as there was never any snacking in between. With an ache in her chest as she remembered home, she picked up some egg on her fork and tried her best to nibble away. Her throat protested and refused to let anything through.

'Stephanie' was embroidered across the chest of a girl who sat directly opposite Nia. She had dark hair and a worried look upon her face. Her face was freckled, and her brows furrowed. She appeared the least anxious of them all, and was attempting, it seemed, to act comfortable. But there was something strange about the way she moved, and the precision with which she cut up her food. The carefulness in which she tucked a single loose strand of hair back into place seemed too artificial, too careful to be at peace.

Nia shifted in her seat and placed down her fork only to pick it back up again.

"I'm Nia," she said quietly, not meaning to startle anyone at the table. There was a hushed atmosphere in the canteen, but other tables were talking and muttering to one another, so Nia had been the one to take the plunge.

From all around their little table of six, each voice piped up one by one and said their name aloud.

"Poppy."

"Matthew."

"Isla."

"Stephanie."

"Charles."

Yes, that is the Charles you think it is. Charles Vanderbilt, the brainy medical genius with the book-smarts to re-set Jay's broken leg during the revolution in what was essentially a tool shed. He did not wear glasses, despite the many magazine comics in later years that featured him wearing a pair of squarely-framed specs – in fact he had remarkable eyesight. His hair was blonde, his eyes were blue, and his face had a roundness to it. The slightly chubby cheeks of childhood, which he had not quite grown out of just yet. Across his cheeks were a smattering of little freckles, and he had a small brown mole on the left side of his forehead. Despite the lacquer on his hair to hold it back, a portion of it insistently shifted forward whenever he looked down, causing a nervous habit of pushing it back whenever he looked up, and rubbing the back of his neck with his palm when it landed there.

This was the moment when Charles and Nia met for the first time. The beginning of a somewhat unlikely friendship, had it not been for the circumstances. Everyone is friends when they're in the same boat – especially when that boat appears to be sinking.

"Do you guys know which troop you're in for classes?" Matthew asked.

"Fifty-three I think, what about you?"

"Thirty-eight."

"I didn't realise there were enough people to make fifty-three troops."

"I've heard there's over fifteen thousand new recruits this year," said Charles, "that's nearly double what they had when my grandpa was here."

"Fifteen thousand? How do they fit everyone in?"

"It's a big campus," Stephanie said, with a somewhat practiced smile. "It's almost the size of a large town."

"Really?"

"Apparently. They've got everything here. They have to make it big if they've got staff and students living here."

"I can't even comprehend how big that is."

"What do you think it's going to be like, living here?"

"I don't know. I don't want to think about it just yet really. I miss home too much right now."

"I can't believe we don't get to go home for three years..."

"We can write."

"Yeah, but it's not the same."

There was a long moment of silence as each of them thought about where they had come from, and the family they had had to leave behind in order to come here.

Nia looked down at her half-eaten breakfast. "I heard it's not a nice place here."

"I heard that too," Poppy added. "I asked my mum about it, but she just went quiet and started to cry. Her sister didn't come back."

"My dad was the same. He didn't want me to go."

"My older brother didn't come back either," added Charles.

"Where do you think they go? Where do they take them?" Isla asked.

"Isn't it obvious?" Matthew said.

There was a very long moment of silence once again.

> Making friends can be a very daunting and tricky matter. This issue is always made easier when those who are talking have something in common that they can associate with one another. Empathy and relatability are always good subjects to open a conversation.

> You must understand how tragic it is though that the only thing these young adults had found they had in common with one another was that each of them had family members who had died, and family members who did not want them to be in the situation I am describing to you. Most of us may have discussed the latest movies, or our childhoods, or even the classes we had later in the day. These kids talked about death as if it were a sorry inconvenience, such as missing the bus, rather than a formidable and ghastly end, like it really was.

It was 07:10 precisely when the clock chimed once more. A calm male voice sounded over hidden speakers overhead, loud and clear:

"Cadets, please proceed to exit four. Your orientation will begin shortly in the Assembly Hall. Lieutenants will be present to guide you. Please ensure your food tray is stored correctly in the racks provided. Exit four, please proceed."

Each exit was clearly labelled. Exits one to three led towards the dormitories in Nia's block, and four to six were the exits of the building itself, spaced evenly throughout the large canteen. Nia took her half-eaten breakfast and placed it on the rotating shelving unit, which carted away the trays to be cleaned somewhere behind a wall. Among others, and with Charles and Stephanie and Isla and Matthew and Poppy, Nia stood in line and marched briskly with the rest out into the chill air of the morning.

The sun was still rising as they walked and was golden and bright through the rising mist. It was blinding in places, causing Nia to squint. She noticed frost in places. It twinkled on windowsills and grass on the training fields. The concrete beneath her shoes felt hard and cold. As they walked, she could see everyone's breath climb into the air.

For one short moment, Nia thought maybe this place was not too bad. She thought perhaps all they had been saying to them was true after all – this place really could be a fresh start for everyone. This might just be the beginning of their lives that they had been waiting for.

But then, across the fields, she saw a group of cadets completing an assault course. She saw another group being forced to fight in combat with their fists. Nia presumed they must be Second or Third Years.

Nia saw one girl get whacked in the face and fall to the floor. Blood spewed from her broken teeth and her hot panting formed white clouds in the air as she tried to catch her breath.

The girl was approached by the group's lieutenant. A man. He was shouting at her to get up, to fight back. The girl protested, clutching her face, and crying.

The lieutenant pulled her up by the hair. He roughly shook her and yelled at her some more. Then, when she still did not comply, he placed a hand on either side of her head and twisted sharply. The girl fell to the floor like a rag doll.

And where Nia had once seen her breathing, she watched the last small puff of her white breath float into the air and dissipate as if it had never been there at all.

Nia sharply turned away to face the person ahead of her. She pretended she had not seen what was now replaying over and over in her head.

It was dark here, even with the golden sun. And Nia knew it would forever be cold, regardless of the season.

She knew right then in that moment that this school, this academy, this training camp would never be a place of safety for her. Her gut twisted inside her, and she knew the truth that had always been so plain, and yet so horrifically hidden.

People died here.

Those who did not do as instructed, those who did not become the people they were instructed to be – those people did not go home.

CHAPTER THIRTEEN

124 DAYS BEFORE

Bella Lockett had kept up her façade for her entire life. For twelve years she had studied the world with watchful eyes, and the knowledge that something was wrong. She had done as instructed by her father. She had kept quiet whenever she was around anyone except her own parents. At school she did not fit in with the other children and was not invited into the games they played. They found it odd how she did not talk, or sing, or laugh with them, and so they decided to not let her join in at all – it was their way of approaching the situation in a way that they had control.

But the teachers certainly loved her. She was a student who was quiet and studious and spoke only when instructed to. She did her work to a marvellous standard and, best of all, she did not ask questions. Little did they know that the still outer waters did not reflect the storm that was brewing beneath the surface.

Bella's father, like herself, also did not quite agree with the changing face of the world. He had observed, like so many silent others, how it was unfair and restrictive. He knew that any chance he held of changing the way things were, was now long gone. However, he saw the roaring flames within his daughter's heart, and knew that she might just harbour the potential spark needed to form a revolution against the Dictator.

Mister Lockett's ideas were certainly modern, and undoubtedly classed as treason. But he had no way of implementing them in the minds of the many. All others his age were too barren and set hard in their ways, as if the laws of the times were chiselled deep into their very core.

But the minds of the young – they were still malleable, like clay before it had been given chance to set. It was still possible to mould them into any shape imaginable. To change the starting points of their lives and, in doing so, change the world.

And so, Bella's training began much earlier than her peers'. It was different, too – and it began in the old rotting shed in the far corner of their land, when Bella was just six years old.

Bella stood in the small room, listening to the rain bouncing loudly on the tin above her head as it tried to get in. Despite its efforts, only one little leak *drip-drip-dripp*ed into an empty tin bucket in the corner. There was nothing much in the shed. She remembered it smelled funny. Damp and cold and sour. Sharpened steel knives and axes hung from the walls, covered in dry and crusted blood, ready to be cleaned. When the weather bustled against the wooden walls, the metal would clink and jingle, like an ominous mobile above a baby's crib.

Six-year-old Bella saw a table with a bucket on top which she was too small to see the top of. Feathers littered the floor. Black feathers, brown ones and crisp little white ones. Bella picked one up. It was soft in her hand. She liked it.

Then her father entered, drenched and dripping from the rain. His boots clomped on the floor, caked in fresh mud. His grey hair was slick on his forehead, his shirt and jeans dark from the water. Little droplets hung off his nose. His face was one of seriousness, and in his hands, upside down, he held a chicken.

The bird was oddly tranquil. It hung there as if hypnotised and perplexed at seeing the world from such a new and unusual angle. Its little eyes and head twitched about slightly, but she did not flap, just softly clucked.

"Chicken!" Bella said, waving her feather in the air. But her daddy did not smile, nor even give her a smirk. Not today.

He plonked the chicken in the bucket on the table. He then

moved a stool from the corner of the room. Down went the stool, on went Bella. The room looked even bigger from up there.

Bella saw the chicken clucking about in the bucket. She was confused now and did not know what was going on.

"Bella," he said, "I'm going to ask you to do something in a moment, okay? And I don't think you're going to like it. But it must be done, if you want to be a brave person and change the world one day. Do you understand?"

Bella did not understand, but she nodded, nonetheless.

He took a large metal blade from off the wall and placed it in Bella's tiny hand. It was heavy, and very sharp, but she found to her own surprise that she could lift it on her own.

"You got that?" Papa asked.

Again, she nodded.

Father then took the bucket and moved it closer. He took out the white fluffy hen and placed her on the table.

"What I need you to do Bella, is lift up the blade, hold it over the bird's neck, here –" He pointed to where he meant, "– and then bring it straight down, hard and fast, okay? I'll hold her still for you."

"But dada, I don't want to kill the chicken."

"I know, darling," he said, "but one day, the Authorities are going to ask you to do all kinds of things, and some of them might be much worse than this. And darling, if you don't do it, then they will kill *you*."

Her father was trying to be gentle, but there was only so much one could do when training a child to do such a horrible thing.

"But *why* do I have to kill the chicken? Why will they make me do bad things?"

"Because they are bad people, sweetheart. Do you remember when I asked you if you wanted to change the world and you said 'yes'? Well this is a part of that. And one day, when you are saving the world, you will have to kill a bad person. You might have to kill a lot of bad people. But it is for the greater good of all the people who live on after us. Wouldn't you like to be able to talk at school, and grow up to be whoever you want to be? Doesn't that freedom sound exciting?"

"But dada..."

"No, Bella. Do it."

Bella protested and cried, and her papa raised his voice. They could not be heard here amidst the rain, so Bella could scream and yell in protest as much as she wanted.

But her father was done being nice and was having none of it. There was a deep sadness in his heart, but he knew that he must be firm with her. It was for her own good – he repeated this to himself, tired of the weight of the world and the anguish he felt for his young daughter's future. It was for her own good.

"Bella, this is the one and only time I will ever make you do this. Now, do it."

Bella scowled. Her face was hot, her hands shook, and she saw too many similarities between her father and the teachers at school. She was being made to do things she did not want to do.

She brought down the knife with a quiet *thunk*, and her father shoved the dead bird upside-down in the bucket to drain it of the blood. Bella stared at the ghastly red table and the chicken's severed head, looking back at her.

"I do not like you for this, papa."

"I know," he said quietly. "But one day, when you are free to say that to anyone you wish, and are treated equal to your fellow men, you will thank me."

Bella did not understand. Twelve years later she still thought about that moment and realised how it had all pieced together. She had never killed or eaten another chicken in that time, but she *had* killed a handful of people – only a small handful. And she would probably not have been able to do it had it not been for her father's grim training methods.

Her father looked down at her sad face.

"I'm proud of you," he said, as he hugged her. She sobbed onto his shirt with a fierceness that made his heart ache. "Now, what do we say?"

"Long live the revolution!"

It all began on a humble chicken farm in the middle of the countryside. It started a revolution. It lasted for years. The story of how one fiery red-haired girl changed the world.

CHAPTER FOURTEEN

124 DAYS BEFORE

Veronika Shaw. She was a Second Year cadet. Known by her classmates as one to be feared, and by her friends as one to be trusted. She was the perfect balance between teacher's pet and brave volunteer. She had found just exactly where 'the line' was and had not dared to put a single boot lace over it. There, she found she was favoured by all. The head girl of her troop – her entire year. Academically talented, socially loved, and professionally skilled.

Veronika Shaw was, in her own words, a survivor. She did whatever it took to get by, to be safe, and she did this well. A talented chameleon in a hostile and intense environment. An adaptor to change.

Veronika had been one of the smart few who hacked the system early on and was dedicated and fierce-minded enough to see it through. She had learned very quickly not to get attached to anything, or anyone. Once you felt love towards something – a dorm room, a belief, a friend – it made it so much more hurtful when that thing was eventually taken away.

The key to her success was simple. Adapt to change, don't get attached, and accept where you are.

That way, she had no weaknesses. Plus, the Government had, theoretically, no good reason to touch her.

It was the first day of the second year of her training. Veronika and her troop were doing their morning physical drill, including a lap around the camp's exercise field. Veronika was the only one in her troop not to produce noises of disdain or exhaustion as they ran.

Adapt to change, don't get attached, accept where you are.

The run was mandatory. Complaint would only make it last longer. She into a rhythm.

They had made it to the back wall of the track. Here was the closest you could get to the outside world. All that could be seen beyond was trees. But no one knew how dense the forest was, or where it led. No one would ever know. No one made it over that wall without being shot in the head first.

There was still evidence from the last escape attempt towards the left corner of the gigantic wall. A bloodied handprint, smeared downwards, and the barbed wire strung in a mess towards the ground, rather than neatly spiralling over the top of the eight-foot wall. Veronika was very aware that on the opposite side of the bricks lay the fresh corpse of a boy who should have been running with the rest of the troop that day. The stress had been too much for him. He was shot four times in the chest before he eventually collapsed. Clearly the fate he chose for himself was preferable to living a life decided for him.

Veronika continued to run. She sped up until she was ahead of the rest, her strides long, her forehead sweating – sprinting faster and farther than she needed to.

She longed so desperately to escape from this place. But she longed ever more to survive. All evidence suggested that both dreams could never exist together simultaneously.

The morning passed her in a series of blips, as she went through the physical routine.

Chest out, shoulders back, feet together, stomach in.

Most important was to retain an alert, yet not overly responsive, expression.

We are nothing but things to them. She heard her mother's

voice in her head and tried to shake it out again.

She raised her hand, she saluted, she yelled the usual responses to the lieutenant's questions.

She ran the assault course, hauled herself over the obstacles, under netting, through thick mud that desperately clung to her. Swimming, climbing ropes, lifting weights. All the while witnessing the male assault course alongside and longing to take part in their weight training.

And then, the combat fighting.

Survive.

The girl she was up against today looked so timid in front of her, so weak, so tired, so afraid. Veronika did not wish to hurt her.

"Begin!"

Vern grabbed the girl's hair and manoeuvred her into a headlock. She used her free fist to pound once into her stomach, the second into her mouth, before tripping her ankle and watching her collapse.

Survive.

The girl doubled over and flopped to the floor, her teeth now red with the blood. She was sobbing. Veronika knew better than to help her up.

"Again!" shouted the lieutenant.

The girl shook her head, clutching her jaw. Veronika had felt it crunch. It was broken.

The lieutenant was having none of it.

"*Again!*" he said once more. The girl's broken teeth prevented her from speaking. She gargled and mumbled, and spat out the blood. But she did not move.

"Get up!" yelled the lieutenant. "Get up and fight, you useless bag of shit! We're preparing for a war here!"

The girl protested and sobbed, clutching her face.

"You dare disobey me?!" He lunged at her and grabbed her by her hair, dragging her up.

"Fight! Fight, you stupid bitch, FIGHT!"

The girl just sobbed. She was not going to fight Veronika.

That was the exact reason she hadn't hit her to begin with. It had been too easy.

"Did you not hear me or somethin'? I said: FIGHT!" He began to shake her in his fury. He screamed in her face. He yanked on her hair.

"But... *why?*" the girl mumbled.

The lieutenant stopped, going red in the face, and dropped her onto her feet. He laughed, once, evidently unamused. Then, in one short motion, he lunged forward and grabbed her firmly by her shoulders and head. He twisted sharply, and broke her neck.

Veronika kept her gaze straight ahead, not wanting to see the girl on the ground.

The rest of the group had been stunned into silence.

"Does anyone else have any intention of pissing me off today?"

The silence remained. Veronika could feel the girl's lifeless eyes looking at her from the ground.

"Well? Do you?"

"No, sir!" the chorus of voices answered. They raise their hands in a respectful salute.

"Good. Next pair. You're up."

Veronika returned to the line. Her gaze returned to the dead girl, whose body had not been removed from the small grassy area. She looked so delicate, so innocent. That morning she had woken up, gone through her usual routine, and had probably presumed she would be returning to her bed later that day.

If she was lucky, her body would be respectfully cremated, and her family told. If not, her remains would simply be hauled over the wall and left to rot. The smell would be left to linger on the field whenever the wind blew, as a reminder to the rest. Her parents would not be told either. On Returns Day, a year from now, they would be waiting with all the other parents to greet her. When they ask a member of staff where their daughter was, they would be told there was no record of her.

She never existed.

Later that day, upon returning to her room, Veronika looked at her reflection in the bathroom mirror. Her shiny black hair was pulled back neatly in several braids, her dark skin was smooth and without imperfections. Her brown eyes were hard and empty, as they were in front of others. But on days like today, she liked to watch herself crumble. Just for a few minutes, just while she grieved. She clutched the porcelain sink with both hands and sobbed into the basin of soapy water.

She hated it here, in times like these, and thought about the dead girl as she washed the tearstains from her cheeks. Veronika would never know what happened to her body or her family.

She dried her face with a towel and gave herself a small inner talking to.

Don't get attached to anything, Veronika. Survive.

CHAPTER FIFTEEN

110 DAYS BEFORE

It was in the early evening, two weeks after their induction, when Bella finally plucked up her courage and approached Ardenia Galloway properly. She had spent the entire fortnight searching for others who shared her way of thinking, to no success. Rebels did not often make themselves known. She would need Nia's help if she was to save the world and discover more young cadets who were just like her.

Bella knew about the cameras and watchful eyes that filled every room and corridor. She'd known that every dorm room contained a clock before she had even set foot in one. It was almost common but unspoken knowledge that the Governmental cameras placed on the streets, in shops, and in homes, were not there to protect them. They were there to ensure nobody stepped out of line.

Her father was a smart man and had managed to keep his true thoughts cleverly concealed throughout his life. He was trusted enough to be given a job on the outskirts of The Territory, and to be checked on only semi-annually.

They had been fortunate enough that cameras and microphones were situated only in the house, and not in Mister Lockett's custom-built workshop. He had brought up the idea with a member of authority at an opportunistic moment during an annual visit. This was shortly after Bella was born. He had strategically suggested that his working outside was not necessarily the best for the business, nor the country. The blood was attracting foxes, which were distressing the chickens and affecting the produce.

"So, build a shed, set traps, lock them away. And use the fox fur you gain for warmth. We are further rationing the coal next month."

"I certainly will, sir," Mr Lockett said, rather humble.

Bella had been taught her father's manipulative ways, whilst still retaining the humble and weak exterior that was expected of women. Men, particularly those in Authority, liked to believe that things were their own ideas, and not that of others. The two of them had used her father's tiny camera-free shed to conspire and to plan and to learn. Bella had memorised floor plans of each building and had used the tour of the grounds that morning at Camp Clandestine to solidify her mental pictures. She knew what a hidden camera looked like, and how to find one - as well as how to then disable it. She was also developing her skills on seeing through the false submissive exterior of those who truly longed to be free, like her.

She looked as calm and collected as she could that evening, with her white binder clutched under her arm, and her long hair tucked neatly behind her ears. Bella left her dorm room and headed down the corridor.

It looked old and worn. It did not matter if the wallpaper was an off-green, or that the floorboards were a dark brown, or that the pictures of famous fallen warriors lined the hallways in red frames. To Bella, at least, they were all overshadowed by their own old, untrue motives. She doubted that half the portraits were of real people. Propaganda was one of their most prominent tactics. It would be easy for them to create fake oil paintings of non-existent heroes for the young ones to model themselves on. Unrealistic role models to achieve un-humanistic dreams.

The dorm rooms were very much laid out in the style of apartment blocks. Bella walked to the end of the corridor and turned left, to find the lift. The metal grate gleamed a beautiful newly-polished gold – recently cleaned by a young cadet – and Bella pulled them back and stepped inside. She closed the two behind her, and pressed the button for the twelfth floor.

The lift jittered before sliding downwards with steady ease. Bella watched the floor she had just been standing on pass up above her head and disappear from sight. A little golden bulb lit the tiny space. She could sense it was also the home to a tiny, electronic eye.

The lift clattered to a stop, and Bella opened the grates with a quiet squeak, being sure to shut them again behind her.

Her feet were silent on the flooring as she searched for room 1242. The room of Ardenia Galloway.

FAUX PAS (N.)

An embarrassing remark or action in a social situation.

The information pack that each cadet was given on their first full day at Camp Clandestine came in a large white leather folder.

Inside was enough reading material sufficient to write a book of holy teachings. Of course, there was no longer such thing as religion. The Government's aims were to erase any hope in anything but themselves. There's was the only way to survive.

There was a map of the premises – a detailed map – and further instructions on how to navigate between buildings. There were telephone numbers, staff names and pictures, a uniform list, a code of conduct, a reading list. Illustrations of how to perform a correct salute, an assignment list with relevant deadlines. There were class lists, syllabus specification outlines, daily exercise routines, dinner schedules, stationary requirements, declaration forms. A test on common knowledge, a written IQ test, a mathematics test, a literary task, a medical form. A personal identification card and accompanying number. A small pot of pills (including a daily vitamin supplement, an extra protein supplement for improved recovery and strength-building, and a birth-control pill for the females), and the all-important monthly itinerary.

The itinerary took up most of the bulk. It was essentially a final, printed copy of each cadet's life for the next four weeks. The following month they would get another, and so on and so forth. It contained a detailed list of daily expectations, from wake to sleep, which each cadet was expected to follow. Cardio, strength building, shooting practice, physical training, academics, independent study, recreation, eating, sleeping, washing, and many other daily activities.

It served as a help book to each cadet so that they felt more secure in their environment. It also meant they had somewhere safe to look for answers, and thus theoretically progress throughout their training at a more accelerated rate. This of course, was not always the case. But I find it a nice touch that they made even the tiniest effort to actually take the cadets' state of mind into account.

What they did not realise, however, was that the extent of information they had provided was dangerously in-depth.

I say dangerously, because the Authorities were so distracted with setting up their little scheme and giving their workers a life raft, that they forgot how being too helpful does not always fall in one's favour.

Surely if you were scared someone would come after you, or escape from your giant mandatory hell-hole of a boot camp, you wouldn't want to give them a giant binder. Especially one which provided them with the fundamental visual ai s in starting a revolution – such as, the photographs and con ict details of your staff, a copy of the rule book, and a huge detailed map of the premises.

But I'm just an investigator. Don't take my word for it.

CHAPTER SIXTEEN

110 DAYS BEFORE

Nia sat at her desk, with only the lamp for light. She leafed through the huge white leather binder and its contents.

Whilst she had been out that day, another uniform had made an appearance in her room. Physical training and combat gear. The uniform consisted of black trousers, and matching weatherproof jacket, a white vest for warmth and, underneath, where it hung on the wardrobe door – black combat boots, in her exact size. She was unsure whether to find their extensive knowledge of her impressive, or alarming. At no point had she been measured or asked for her dress size.

The uniform stared at the back of her head while she sat at her desk. Upon studying the schedule for the following day, she was very aware that she was going to be wearing it tomorrow. Or, rather, it was going to be wearing her. She imagined its embroidered sleeves encasing her body in darkness, and itchy elastic cuffs gripping onto her skin. She shuddered.

The binder was, as they had been warned, extensively detailed. She had read the introduction, her schedule for the coming month, and the basic preparatory sheets of information she thought she would need to know for the following day. There was a great deal to take in and remember. And a great deal more that she was expected to know as soon as possible.

She noted that each piece of writing followed the same

similar message:

You are lesser than us, and you will do as we say. Your purpose is to serve us. Do not betray this trust, or we will punish you. Do not forget that it is not illegal for us to kill you.

It was a stressful read. She glanced behind her at the great clock face.

Time spent in servitude will make a man rich.

Nia began to think servitude may not be quite as ideal as everyone was making it out to be. It was an old word, a word not used often anymore. Nia did not know why, but she wondered whether the original meaning of it had not been good.

> It wasn't. You may find it difficult to believe a Government had managed to produce and enforce an entirely different dictionary upon an entire population of people, but it happened. And back when Nia was alive, servitude really did mean 'the serving of others out of love.' I know. Crazy. But true.

Knock-knock-knock.

Each beat was precise and with intention.

Nia stood and straightened her skirt, pushing her shoulders down. She had not been expecting visitors.

She walked over and swung open the door – and there she was. The way Bella looked made her feel vulnerable.

Nia found it quite a shock to see her there, in her smart uniform and bright red lipstick. She jumped and stiffened as soon as the door swung open.

"Why are you here?" Nia said, rather rudely. Her face gave away her panic.

"Oh, I'm so glad you asked," Bella answered, "I've just been looking through my binder, and I'm a little stuck on one of the assignments. Would you mind explaining it to me better?"

"What?"

"The assignment, the introductory test. There's a question I don't understand."

"Okay..."

"If you bring your binder I was just going to sit downstairs and do some work. Please, come with me."

"Actually, I—" Nia tried to protest, but the girl had already scooted past her. She was now at Nia's desk, picking up her binder. Bella looked out of place in her room. It made Nia feel uncomfortable that she was there, at her desk.

"Who are you?"

"Bella Lockett," she said, extending a hand. Nia shook it distractedly, out of habit. "And you are Ardenia Galloway, yes?"

"Uh... yes?"

"Well, come now. I know a good place where we can study together. I'm so excited to learn more about what our futures hold here at the camp, aren't you?"

And with a white folder tucked under each arm, she left the room, and began to wander towards the staircase. She was either oblivious that Nia wasn't yet following her, or knew that she eventually would.

Locking her door behind her, she followed. Nia would not survive her years at Camp Clandestine without her binder. She had no choice.

Bella said very little to Nia on the walk downstairs. She knew where they were going, but no matter how many times Nia asked, she did not get a straight answer.

"Don't you know it's not good for you to ask too many questions? My mother would always say that everybody has a predetermined number of questions they could ask in their life time. And that if you ask too many questions then your ears will fall off and your tongue will fall out, and you'll never be able to speak again!"

Obediently, Nia quietened. They walked down the remaining steps.

They were the only ones around. Their footsteps echoed. Nia felt her heart pound again. Bella could have been leading Nia to her death, for all she knew. Yet she continued to willingly follow. She wanted to presume that being on a premises with so many cameras would protect her. But what she had witnessed in the past few weeks did not have her quite thoroughly convinced. If her companion chose to kill her, it was doubtful that anyone would care. Nia was, effectively, a nobody. Just another face among the masses.

Bella stopped. They had reached the bottom.

She stood still for a moment and closed her eyes – listening.

"We're clear – this way," Bella said.

She opened one of the double doors on the opposite side of the corridor to the stairs. The black void it opened into was mysterious and shook Nia to the core. The cafeteria at night was certainly an entirely different place.

Bella entered. Nia felt she could do nothing else but follow her into the unknown.

Nia's eyes did not adjust for some time, as the door swung slowly shut behind her. She watched the white sliver of light get smaller and smaller until it was gone. It was so dark, she could see nothing, at first. Her eyes were wider than they'd ever been before. Nia heard Bella place the binders on a table. Nia headed slowly towards the sound. As she walked forward, she began to make out the edges of her surroundings – the rows of identical metal tables and benches, aligned perfectly in ten rows by too many columns to count. A loud *clack* broke the silence, as Bella opened one of the metal window shutters. Moonlight from the clouded night sky above leaked down. Whatever it was that this girl was about to shed some light would be important. Their fates, she somehow knew, were bound.

"Sit down, this has to be quick. If anyone comes in, say we couldn't find the light switch, okay?"

Nia nodded. "Okay," she said, after realising that she probably couldn't be seen. "What is this about? Are you here to fix me? Y'know, because you think I'm... "

"Fix you?" She laughed. "I forgot how twisted they make you guys. Pal, I'm not here to change you back to fit their tiny little boring moulds. I'm here to help you get out of the mould that you don't fit into and teach you how to break it without them realising. Then, I'll teach you how to help *me* help the *others*."

"What? Are you *crazy*?" Nia said. "Change? Don't you know what saying that word will do to you if they find out? What if they hear you?" Nia stood up, confused as to why Bella seem so determined to get them both killed?

"They can't hear us, not in here. No microphones. I checked this room this morning. It's too loud at mealtimes to hear anything," she said quietly. "You're in too deep already, Nia, you know that. If you leave now, you're on your own with this secret, with the knowledge that you are Curious leeching away at you in everything you do, driving you mad, like it did to Doctor Schiffer –"

"What do you know about…?"

"– and you'll also never learn what I have to say, what I have to suggest. And I think *that* is what will distress you the most. Because a part of you already knows that my suggestions will be the only chance you have to live a life that you are in control of, and to get out of here before they kill you."

Nia stopped and studied her silhouette in the darkness. She sat back down. Everything Nia had ever learned was telling her she should run, that she should lock her bedroom door, she should report Bella Lockett and her Curious ways.

But something deeper, something innate, something in her gut was insisting that she sat down, and that she listened.

"Alright," Nia said quietly, "I will listen to what you have to say. But I warn you now, if I don't like what you tell me, I will have no choice but to tell the Authorities."

"Trust me," Bella replied, sitting down opposite her, "you will want to hear what I have to say."

CHAPTER SEVENTEEN

110 DAYS BEFORE

E ddie swung his legs over the edge of his bed and rubbed the back of his neck. It wasn't yet too late, but it was certainly dark outside.

Eddie quite liked the night. It was a still time of day, with no distractions, few expectations, and more hours than many people realised. A lot of living can be done when everyone else in the world is in a state so similar to death.

He spread his toes and stretched his ankles. Walked naked and barefoot towards the mirror over the dresser.

"You can go," he said, making eye contact with only his reflection until she had exited the room.

He saw in his peripheral vision the reflection of the naked girl as she covered herself in a scarlet robe and collected her things. She was exceptionally quiet, maddeningly submissive, and it riddled him with guilt from inside to out.

"Laura," he said, quietly.

She froze and stood up straight with one hand on the doorknob.

"Come back in three days." His voice was thick. He saw the back of her head dip low to the ground, and she disappeared into the hallway like a shadow.

Eddie looked back into his own blue eyes. He hated everything he saw. The silver tags around his neck held his name, but he no longer felt like they matched his own face anymore. There was a dullness in his eyes now – a darkness. He could see it. It had been seeping into him ever so slowly as each year passed. The things he had witnessed, the things he had been forced to do by his father's hand, by the Dictator's orders. They had begun to blanket his eyes with a film. A hidden mist. Others would call him mad, but he could see it, there, in the mirror. Every dark deed he partook in the veil grew thicker. It was an addictive form of misery. He knew the cause, he knew the consequence, but for some reason – be it submission, or selfish greed – he could not help but satisfy the itch.

He had been trained to develop these skills, these habits. He had been habituated to enjoy the cold company of uninterested and fearful lovers and the feeling of the warmth of another's blood on his own clenched knuckles. His peers, his elders, all those who surrounded him, took part in these activities. They praised them, taught them, worshipped them. Eddie had been raised to do so, too.

But something about it just felt so very wrong, so incredibly twisted. It made him want to recoil, look away, despite the fact his eyes had been forced open by his father. He had insisted Eddie devour every moment. Insisted blood from another was a sign of power. Insisted resistance from a lover was a sign of passion.

He knew nothing else, but he felt the ideas were wrong. He did not delight in punishing those who disobeyed, or who did not show grand results. He did not find amusement in watching others fight to impress him or hang on his every word. He did not feel his soul dance when kissing a girl who grimaced, or who asked his permission to leave. Yet this was what happened – a daily occurrence.

He walked over to the window of his bedroom, gazing out into the night. He watched Laura in her robe shivering as she walked back across the courtyard to her dorm. It was at night he felt he was completely alone. He felt allowed to run away with his thoughts, and relax back into the person he knew he really was. It was simply a shame that the safety of the night had to end, and the morning would come once more, expecting his greatest charade yet again.

He turned back to his bed, and planned to rest before the sun peeked through the dismal clouds. But just as he did so, he saw a shutter in the First Year cadets' canteen room being pulled open. He could just make out the silhouettes of two figures sitting there, in the dark.

He did not ponder too much about what they were doing. He found his clothes, he dressed, and he made for the door – not because he was furious, but because he was anxious not to allow another lieutenant to get there first.

As he walked, the veil over his eyes began to lift.

CHAPTER EIGHTEEN

110 DAYS BEFORE

"The Government's main goal is to extinguish any threat to them, and the power they already hold over us," Bella explained. "Curious Folk, like you and I, are a prime example of such a threat. We are of young mind, and therefore highly susceptible to new ideas and rebellion. The Dictator and the Government fear Curious Folk, because all it takes is one person to plant an idea in the head of ten more people, and the idea will spread. That's why they describe Curiousness as a disease. They don't want us to ask questions, they don't want us to realise we have the right to be free, because if one of us gets the idea that we should have the right to decide our own future, our own fate, then they have already lost everything that they have taken so long to build."

She blinked, and Nia was taken aback slightly by her intenseness. Her head was spinning with all the information it had just gained in approximately ninety seconds.

"It's a complex structure," Bella continued, "with so many layers of security and surveillance that some may think it foolproof... But it is also a delicate structure. It has only been introduced fully in the last ten years, and so they are continuing to work out the kinks. We need to take advantage of that fact, because right now they are certain that they are relatively safe. They think by pushing the prime age group for Curious Folk into an army base and watching and controlling them twenty-four-seven that they've cracked it. They don't think we'd dare try anything – and that's the exact reason why this is the perfect place to make our plan."

"Plan?" Nia asked. "Plan for what?"

"Did you not read my note?" Bella laughed. *"Freedom of thought, freedom of life, freedom of expression. Down with the oppression!* A plan to escape. A plan to free everyone, and create a world where we feel safe to go to sleep at night. Safe to say how we think, how we feel. Safe to… love whoever we want to love."

"I don't know if…"

"Don't you get it? Don't you realise what will happen if you don't help me with this? *Nothing!* Nothing happens. We, and all future generations, will just stay trapped in this awful, manipulative system that feeds off our fear, and it will probably get only darker and darker with each year of cadets that comes through here. We must start this, Nia. We must *do* something, even if no one else will. We need to gain support, gain followers, and make the Government piss their pants in *fear.* I can't wait to see the look on their faces when a band of teens with guns and bollocks of steel take down a whole fucking army!"

Her eyes lit up so brightly as she talked. There was so much fire and passion behind everything she said. In Bella's heart, she knew this was the right thing to do. She could feel it. And wow was it catchy. As she spoke, Nia felt what Bella did. She felt her heart swell and lighten, she felt her mind reach a state of euphoric wonder. Nia hung on each of her words and it felt *so good* to imagine, to dream, of such a perfect and bright and wonderful world.

But she and Bella were not the people she was speaking of. Certainly not.

"An army? Bella, we can't take down an army. We've been here for less than a month, and you want me to run away with you and save the world? Are you mad?"

"My father always said there was a fine line between madness and brilliance." She smirked.

"But don't you hear yourself?"

"Don't you hear *your*self?" She scowled. "I've just told you that there's a chance we could change the entire structure of this country for good - improve the futures of *so many* people – and you don't want to hear it? Don't you want that?"

"Of course, I do, but –"

"But you don't want to get your hands dirty and make it happen? You want someone else to make the world perfect for you? Well that's not how it works, Nia. You don't just have things that you want presented to you. Sure, the Government will supply you with a job, a house, a husband – but is it a job you want? A house you love? A partner you adore? No! It's just what you're given. And that's why everybody here is miserable. They're in a job they hate with a spouse they don't want to care for and have sex with, and everyone is too fucking cowardly to do anything about it!"

Nia sat there, shocked, and felt each of Bella's words penetrate her heart. It sounded so mad, it felt so far away, it was certainly too wild a dream.

But, dammit, Nia wanted everything Bella had said. She wanted it. It made so much sense to her.

"Bella, I think–"

There was a loud click. Above them, the lightbulbs pinged to life, making the two girls squint.

"What are you doing in here?"

It was Lieutenant Johnson, dressed in a casual black t-shirt and matching black khakis. He stood strong, fierce and tall, with a stern face. His eyes were a terrifically piercing blue, which only added to his entrancingly petrifying persona.

Nia clutched her binder in her hands until her knuckles were the same colour as it. It was heavy on her lap. She knew it would tie her to the camp like an anchor to the ocean, but it held a sense of order and prediction that she had longed for since the moment she had left her parents' home.

"We were just trying to do some work, sir," Bella said.

"In the dark?"

"We couldn't find the light switch, sir."

He looked between them, then down at the binders, then

back up at their faces. Nia gulped. Her toes curled. She didn't think she could possibly avoid his gaze any more obviously.

"Return to your dorms at once," he said. "Don't let anyone catch you down here again after feeding hours. It could... end badly."

"Yes, sir." Bella nodded. The pair saluted him, then scurried from the room and back up the stairs.

As they walked, Nia sneaked a glance down, and was certain she saw Lieutenant Johnson smirking to himself. She noted what a nice physique he had, and how his smirk made her want to smile herself.

When three floors up, and it was safe to talk again, Bella nudged her and said, under her breath:

"Did you notice how he phrased it?"

Nia looked at her, confused.

"He didn't say we weren't allowed down there. He said don't get caught."

"So?" Nia asked.

"*So,* this is important." She giggled. "I think he's one of us."

MOLE (N.)

1. *A covert human intelligence source planted within an organisation.*
2. *An adorable burrowing creature which lacks the ability to see.*

Bella Lockett was not wrong.

Eddie had known for some time at this point that he was Curious. He had been struggling to come to terms with the idea for almost three years. The risk of revealing to the world who he really was, was simply was not an option. He was the son of one of the most respected men in the armed forces – of the entire *country*. His father met with the Dictator on a regular basis simply to share tea and a cigar. For Eddie to reveal he was an enemy of the state, a traitor, a man in position of command who was not who they believed him to be...

He would be dead before he finished his first sentence.

However, everybody reaches a breaking point. No one can hide who they truly are and how they truly feel for too long. Emotions can only be repressed for a certain amount of time before they either explode, or start to rot their carrier from the inside out. Like an acorn infected by the spawn of a wasp – sucked inwards by the poison it contains.

Eddie was not one to allow himself to rot.

He was waiting for his chance.

In Bella Lockett and Ardenia Galloway, it arrived.

CHAPTER NINETEEN

99 DAYS BEFORE

Nia woke to the striking of the great clock on the wall.

She hadn't told Bella whether she wanted in or not. She felt hesitant, understandably, and Bella agreed to give her some space to think it out.

"Take all the time you need," Bella had said, "I won't stop working towards the goal while you think. You know where to find me."

Less than twelve hours afterwards, and Nia had already been considering it. As each day passed, her passion only grew stronger. The words of both Bella and Suzanne Schiffer kept ringing in her ears...

Was this right?

She felt afraid, because she knew her own opinion would not make much impact either way. She didn't think that they could make that much of a difference. She felt so trapped by her inner world against the outer one. The rules and wants could not be more opposing. Her heart carried a deep sadness that morning. She longed to crawl back under the bedsheets and hide in the dark until it had all gone away. She wanted her youth back. She wanted to run, to jump, without question or reason or goal or order. She wanted to do things that she wanted to do. She wanted to do things that she wasn't expected to do.

But Nia couldn't. None of them could. The clock ticked on.

The time passed by. She had no choice that morning. Get up, get dressed, head out. She had to do as she was told.

That morning, she attended a meeting with the Committee of Employment Advisors.

The office was in the main building. It was the same building where they had watched the propaganda video on the first day. The bricks were strong and old, put together carefully some years ago. It was the oldest, grandest part of campus. This was where the highest members of staff resided, where all the important meetings were held. Cadets could only enter if they had been invited.

In the entrance halls, Nia had been expecting to be greeted by a receptionist, perhaps on the other side of a glass screen. Where a real person would otherwise have been, a place television screen had been placed. It was built into the wall. If it hadn't lit up upon her entering, Nia would have missed it.

The voice that spoke from it was inviting:

"Good afternoon. Please be aware that entrance of cadets into the Grand Halls are by appointment only. Do you have a pre-booked appointment today?"

"Affirmative."

"Please state your name and reason for entry."

Nia did.

"Access granted."

A heavy oak door to her left swung steadily open automatically. The handle, which was unnecessary, was made of gold.

"Please follow the corridor. The offices for the Committee of Employment Advisors is clearly marked. You will find it to be the sixteenth door on your left. Do you require further instruction?"

"Negative."

"Thank you. Have a pleasant day."

As Nia passed through the doorway, it slowly closed behind

her. The corridor she was confronted with had a ceiling higher than she'd ever seen before. Portraits and maps decorated every surface, accented in gold. Nia wondered how an artist could even get up that high with their paintbrush. The corridor gleamed with a warm, expensive light.

True to instruction, Nia found the door. It, too, was heavy and expensive looking.

She knocked once. The response came immediately.

"Enter, Ms Galloway."

Again, the door shut behind her without her needing to touch it.

"Be seated."

There were five of them. Their shared desk was on a platform, so they looked down at where she sat. The lone chair in the centre of the room was average, in every way. But in this room, it felt tiny.

The leader of the committee was a man with a deep, gravely voice. Clean shaven, chunky fingers that scratched his chin, and a mouth that was well practiced at frowning.

"As I'm sure you're aware, this is a quick meeting to discuss the possibilities for your future career." The man sounded bored. "This is a meeting we have with each cadet when they first arrive here, and we will come back to it on several occasions throughout your education to assess your progress." He cleared his throat gruffly and adjusted his glasses. "Here with me today are the Head of Education for each specific sector: Medicine, Agriculture, Military, Technology, and Manufacturing. You will already be aware of what roles exist within each of these sectors. What we would like to know is which you have chosen to be your major focus."

Nia shifted in her seat and gulped involuntarily.

"At present I am interested in all of them, sir."

The five sets of eyes shifted around and looked amongst themselves.

"All of them?"

Another gulp. "Yes."

"It is made quite clear from the start of the educational process that only one sector can be chosen per cadet. And that choice cannot be undone."

The air tensed. The five sets of eyes waited, expectantly.

"I was...hoping," Nia said, as bravely as she could, "to have more time before making my final decision. I am yet to fully learn about the possibilities within each working sector."

The chair of the meeting narrowed his eyes. "Each cadet is called to this meeting to declare what sector they desire to be a part of. It is as a Second Year cadet that they are required to make more finalised choices. Tell me, Ms Galloway. If you cannot make this decision now, out of a meagre five choices, how do you expect to make further decisions down the line?"

Nia was unsure if an answer was expected of her, and so stayed silent. The chair of the meeting continued:

"We require cadets to be decisive. If called forward to the line of duty, you would be put in positions on a great many occasions where you will need to be decisive. This is not something we want you to learn, it is something you are required to be. Coming to this meeting and not knowing what sector you want to work for is not acceptable. Do I make myself clear?"

"Yes, sir."

A clock on the wall ticked, loudly. Nia only just noticed it. The silence stretched longer and longer. There were mutterings amongst the five gowned figures.

"I will ask you again, Ms Galloway. And I will only ask you once: Which of these sectors have you chosen to be your major focus?"

Nia blinked. Her entire life hung in the balance. Her entire trajectory. On one decision, which she felt far less than informed to make.

"Agriculture."

The man gave an unimpressed smirk.

"Excellent." The five members of the committee grabbed their pens and fervently scribbled something on a form in front of them. "That wasn't so hard, was it?"

As if being stared at by five forboding figures wasn't enough, Nia received another reminder of the realness of Camp Clandestine during one of her classes that day.

She was in Information Technology, a room full of computer screens, sat next to a cadet named Dan. Living in a world that claimed to be only at the start of a technological revolution, basic coding and computer skills were essential for all members of society.

As the lesson ensued, Martin, a boy opposite them, did not appear to be paying attention.

Nia was looking at her computer screen. She was trying to make sense of the statistical data analysis task they had been given. She was getting confused by all the seemingly meaningless numbers and letters. Dan, her work partner, was trying his best to assist her.

"...so then if you click menu, and then scroll down to where it says summation – yeah – there should be an option that says... that's the one! Yeah."

"I feel like computer tasks just aren't my forte. Any sort of maths is like a different language to me."

"You're getting there with it. It just takes practice."

"I'm better at stamina training. I reckon I'd be good at shooting, too. Yet to learn that though."

"They teach that next semester, after the winter."

"I wonder why they..."

Nia's voice trailed off as she noticed Martin's computer screen. His software did not look like what she had up on her screen. Martin was typing furiously. Nia couldn't make out exactly what he was doing.

Dan kept his voice low when he spoke next. He had a deep mumble when he spoke normally, so Nia really struggled to hear what he was saying.

"Say again?"

"He's composing an *email*."

Nia's hand drew instinctively up to her mouth. She looked over once more at Martin. His hands skimmed the keyboard so fast they were in a blur. His attention was on nothing but the words appearing on the screen before him.

Nia was unsure of what to do. She wanted to look away, so as not to draw attention to him, but found that her eyes didn't know where else to look. To see someone so clearly avoiding the designated task, but also attempting to contact someone else from outside of the camps - this was *bad*.

Dan, too, looked like he was struggling with what was the right thing to do. He had his head adamantly down, but he was not focusing on his work.

"How has he even managed to do that?" Nia whispered. "I thought the servers prohibited the use of any internet apart from approved sources?"

Dan shook his head, dismissively. "He must have hacked it."

"How does he even have access to email?"

Dan shot Nia a wide-eyed look of annoyance. Without opening his mouth, he had successfully managed to say *shut the fuck up, will you?*

However, Nia heard whispers among the rest of the class. They had noticed. But, thus far, Martin still had not.

It all happened in somewhat of a blur. Nia watched as a hand was raised silently at the front of the classroom. The teacher approached the student. More whispers.

And then a sharp turn of the teacher's head. Eyes of fury, like Nia had never seen before.

Nia didn't think it possible to cross a classroom so large in three strides, but somehow the teacher managed it. She grabbed Martin's chair from underneath him, sending him forward. He knocked his chin on the desk as he fell. Thankfully, it was not hard enough to draw blood.

The teacher told him to stay on the ground as she skimmed the email he had been typing out.

Just as Nia had feared. Martin had been trying to contact

home.

Dan leaned over and whispered to her. "He will have been using the Prohibited Web."

"What does that mean?"

"Well, you know how the regular web is for the use of permitted individuals only?"

"Mmm."

"The Prohibited Web is used by two types of people. Members of the Government, who have granted access. Or outlaws who hack into it. Criminals."

"Oh, fuck."

"Oh, fuck indeed."

Their whispers were cut short.

"Martin Matthias," the teacher hissed, "do you have anything you'd like to say for yourself?"

"I was just trying to contact my dad!" He pleaded, from where he sat on the ground. "I didn't do anything wrong! I just wanted to check he was okay! And let him know I was okay, too!"

"You know full well that you were doing something wrong. Trying to send a secret message to someone outside of the camps? In the middle of my class? On the *Prohibited Web?*"

Martin gulped. "I–"

"It says here you're hating every second of it. Is that true?"

"Um-"

"Well, let me put you out of your misery, Mister Matthias. I know of one way we can send a message to back home for you."

If Nia had blinked, she would have missed it. She watched, aghast, as the teacher pulled a blade out of her pocket and thrust it as hard as she could into Martin's hand. His palm lay flat against the desk, and Nia saw the blade go right through it – right through his hand, and right through the surface of the wood.

Martin screamed. He used his free hand to grab hold of the blade but couldn't prise it free. Nia had to look away as Martin's head was seized and thrust hard against the desk. It happened over and over.

He screamed and he screamed. Until he screamed no more.

The classroom was silent. Not even the sound of typing filled the air. The cadets were unsure whether to look at their computer screens, or at the mess of blood that was left on the desk, dripping onto the floor. Martin's body was slumped on the ground. His hand still lay on the desk, fixed into place.

"Let this be a lesson to all of you," the teacher said, calmly. She yanked her blade free, and the suspended arm slid down. "Don't ever attempt to contact the outside world. The rules are in place for your own protection. As you saw here today – if you break those rules, your protection ceases."

She took a handkerchief from the top drawer of her desk and wiped away the blood from the blade.

"To ensure you have all taken in the lessons learned today to maximum capacity, I have one more task for you to complete," she said. "I would like you to dispose of the mess that has been created here today in my classroom." A smirk. "Hop to it."

Nia and Dan were amongst the six that were in charge of carrying Martin. It was her first time ever being so close to a dead body. Blood dripped from his head as they walked. His eyes rolled back into his head. It made her feel queasy.

They had been instructed to take Martin to the edge of the training field. It was quite a walk from the IT classroom. Students stared as they walked past, and rightly so. Nia watched Martin's head loll about as they carried him. She wanted to support it, so he was carried respectfully, but she couldn't bring herself to cover her hands with his blood.

The others didn't appear especially phased by the task – or if they were, they didn't let it show. Stephanie, the girl from the canteen, was amongst them.

"Are you okay?" Nia asked her, seeing she was a bit peaky.

Stephanie nodded quickly in response and gave a forced

smile.

Upon reaching the wall, they worked together to haul Martin's body over the top. He was not a large man, but it still took the six of them to do it.

As they were walking back, Nia felt a bleak ache in her heart.

"That was awful. I can't believe she did that."

Dan looked down at his hands and then thrust them into his pockets, "Gotta be done though."

"Does it?"

He didn't respond. They each walked back to their dormitories in thoughtful silence.

Later that afternoon, Nia saw a dorm room on her floor being emptied. The list for her corridor had a name scratched off.

Martin Matthias. He had failed. He would not be going home.

CHAPTER TWENTY

99 DAYS BEFORE

The following weeks after her conversation with Bella gave Nia more fuel to her glowing ashes of misery. She walked and marched and saluted every day in a daze. She followed orders and she jogged, and she pushed herself. But it never really filled her with any sense of joy.

The part that saddened her the most was the knowledge that she wasn't supposed to. Camp Clandestine was doing its practiced and perfected dance. Luring its new cadets in with the comfortable train journey, and the reassuring words – only to steadily empty the hearts of them each time they were told to push their chests out and their shoulders back.

Nia was no longer under Clandestine's spell. Every day she was reminded of how easily those above her could snuff her out with nothing more than an accidental twitch of a finger or take her away never to be seen again.

For an instant, she felt the daze lift. She was sat in the canteen, eating lumpy mashed potatoes with watery cabbage, and she felt a shiver ripple down her spine.

It was in moments like these, when Nia remembered that death was ever-presently standing with one icy hand on her shoulder. It was in moments like these that the daze was gone and she could see clearly, if in a slight state of panic.

Sure, you can have nothing physical to lose, nothing else you can give, nothing more that they can take away from you – what would be the harm in standing up for yourself?

But then you witness them destroy someone who is that one step ahead of you on the route to escaping, and it shakes you to your very core. It makes you turn one-hundred-and-eighty degrees and head willingly back to the hard and trying routine that is all laid out and waiting for you.

Maybe being at Camp Clandestine really was better than being nowhere at all?

But, then again, maybe not.

It was the beginning of winter when Ardenia Galloway realised she had made her decision.

She knocked on Bella Lockett's door. When she answered, Nia gripped her by the shoulders.

"Bella. I'm in."

CHAPTER
TWENTY-ONE

67 DAYS BEFORE

Even Charles was not exempt from witnessing the horrors that the Camps held.

He was one of the most studious students within the entirety of Camp Clandestine. He kept his head low. He had been told by the Committee of Employment Advisors that he was an ideal student. He knew exactly which sector he wanted to work in, and his meeting with the committee had lasted less than two minutes. His efficiency was applauded.

It would be incorrect to presume that by keeping one's head low, one was shielded from the awful things that happened in that awful place. Charles was never subject to a beating, to any hardship. But his fellow students were not so lucky.

Mr Barker was their mathematics teacher. He was by no means a strong man. Instead, he stood tall and lean, like a bean-pole, with a sharp nose and an unimpressed expression - as if he had a bad smell lingering in his nostrils. He wore an immaculate red suit as he paced around the classroom that day. The brightness of the colour made Charles' eyes sting.

Mr Barker's shoes made a clean *tap* on the floor with each step. He walked with a pace that made his trip around the classroom seamless. He did not have to stop at each desk when collecting the student's assignment papers. He breezed past, almost as if he were floating.

Silently, with an attempt at a smile that was not returned, Charles handed over his homework assignment. He crossed and un-crossed his ankles under the desk. He had stayed awake far longer than he should have done to finish it. He prayed that when he had his marks returned, they would adequately reflect the time spent on it.

The footsteps ceased.

"Stephanie Brownlee," Mr Barker said. His voice was icy. "Your assignment?"

Charles, like many others in the room, turned to look.

Stephanie had sat with Charles in the cafeteria on the first day. Just as she had been on that first morning, Stephanie moved with a precision and grace that was laced with over-effort.

Charles noted how tired she looked. Her eyes were round and wide. She blinked often. When confronted by Mr Barker, she visibly stiffened.

"I'm afraid that I..." She issued a mumble that Charles couldn't make out. But he didn't need to hear it to know what was said.

Without a word, so quick that it made everybody in the room jump, Mr Barker reached out a long beanpole arm and struck Stephanie across the face, as hard as he possibly could.

"*UNACCEPTABLE,*" he hissed in her face. "*Finish* it. And get it to me by the end of the day. Understood?"

Stephanie remained silent. She bit down on her quivering lip, a hand pressed against her cheek. She nodded.

"Has anybody *else* in this class failed to do what was asked of them?"

There was an awkward shake of about thirty heads.

"And will anybody *else* be forgetting to bring their completed assignments to me in the future?"

Another chorus of shakes. The odd mumble of *No, sir.*

"Good. Let me see that this remains to be the case."

Mr Barker continued his pacing around the room. His long strides were accompanied by the clean *tap* of his polished shoes as he walked.

Charles looked down at his desk as Mr Barker walked past him. But he couldn't help but look out of the corner of his eye across the room, to where Stephanie sat.

Shielded by a curtain of dark hair, her face was scrunched up tightly. She cried silently, too scared to make a sound.

CHAPTER TWENTY-TWO

67 DAYS BEFORE

She was sweating. The inside of her was too hot, but the outside felt far too cold. Nia and her troop, led by Lieutenant Johnson, were running their first full circuit of the field without stopping. They were only halfway when Nia's lungs felt ready to give up on her. Despite that fact, she was relishing in it. It had been roughly a month since she and Bella had begun their partnership and plans. And part of that realisation was that if they wanted to escape, they needed to be at the peak of physical fitness. Nia had a goal and so with every step she was pushing herself. With each week, she felt her stamina getting tougher and her legs getting stronger. She was feeling something.

"Keep up the good work, team!" the lieutenant yelled. "In a year from now you'll be running around the perimeter of the base, so do not cheat yourself on this now. Do you hear me? *Do not stop.*"

Others would call her crazy to say it but, in comparison to the other leaders, Lieutenant Johnson wasn't that bad. In the past month or so she had grown rather fond of his teaching methods, and the gentle encouragement that he used whilst they trained. She guessed he was one of the younger commanders on the base, but that wasn't why she had an element of warmth towards him. He just seemed more genuine than the rest, more real. Not nice, not empathic, just human. There was a person buried deep in there, and at times during casual conversation either during or after class, Nia had seen a glimpse of the real Lieutenant Johnson – if what Bella had said about him had been true, Nia was set on attempting to dig him out.

That morning she felt brave. She wanted to impress herself with her own abilities and tap through the crusty exterior the lieutenant was portraying. She pushed on and tried her hardest to speed up.

"The trick with bettering yourself, especially with exercise, is to keep going even when your mind wants to give up," Lieutenant Johnson shouted from the front. "Your minds are delicate yet amazingly powerful things. The way we think designs our entire existence, and the way we see the world. If you embrace the heat and the struggle of this practice, and encourage yourselves to see this as a challenge, not a task, you will be amazed at how quickly you will improve. That is also the best way to approach your lives here at this training facility. If you see our teaching and your training as opportunities, you will come to realise how fulfilling a life in servitude to the Government really is."

Nia took a breath. Her head had been filled with these thoughts for some time now. She wanted to know if Lieutenant Johnson really was on the side of Bella and the revolution. She knew she had to get him alone and ask.

"Sir, I feel sick," Nia said. She had managed to catch up with him, and clutched at his arm, desperately.

He looked sharply at her, shocked by her touch, and his pace slowed. "Are you alright?"

"No, sir." She stopped, doubled over and collapsed onto her knees. She dragged the lieutenant's arm down with her. "Something about all this just doesn't feel right to me."

His face was very close to hers and, with her heart trembling at her own bold move, she winked at him.

"Slow your pace!" Eddie shouted to the troop, and everyone stumbled to a stop, hot breath visible in the chill air. Nia watched Lieutenant Johnson straighten himself and address the small crowd. "All of you are to do a few stretches here, and then carry on with the remainder of the run. I shall be escorting Private Galloway to a medical examination. She has over-exerted herself, it would seem."

Nia was sure to hold a pained expression until the other members of her troop had journeyed on. Her grip on Eddie's arm, however, did not cease.

Nia was half-dragged to what looked like an office. A tiny room in one off the changing buildings, stacked floor to ceiling with metal filing cabinets. It felt cold in the room, despite its tiny breathing space. Having not been told anything, Nia wasn't entirely sure what to expect from this. As she was flung into the room by a whipping of the lieutenant's arm, she collided unexpectedly with one of the cabinets with a loud *thwack* – her face whacking against the chill metal with a violent ferocity. She scratched her cheek on the sharp corner of it. Nia pressed her back against the cabinet, seeing it as a form of protection and safety. She did not dare to open her mouth until Lieutenant Johnson had opened his.

She watched him quietly and deliberately close the door behind them. Her heart beat loudly and inconveniently in her ribcage. Apparently it too longed to be free from its prison, with the gusto at which it was beating to get out. She begged it to quieten. But, like a rebellious outlier, it would not listen to its commands.

"What was that about?" he said.

Nia stood, and said nothing. She found strength enough to look back and match his gaze, but not enough to answer him. It didn't need to be spoken. Nia was certain that he already knew what she meant.

"What is your name?" Lieutenant Johnson asked, quietly.

"Galloway, sir," Nia answered, standing tall as best she

could.

"No. Your real name. Your forename."

"Ardenia, sir," she answered. "Known by most as Nia."

He stood closer to her, and Nia realised he wasn't altogether too much taller than she was. A half foot, perhaps, but not much. Still, in a cold quiet room surrounded by sharp-cornered metal boxes, she was certainly still intimidated.

"Nia," he began, "what was it you were wanting to ask me, a few moments ago?"

"I wasn't asking, sir."

"Then what were you doing? Because you clearly are not sick." His expression was like stone – unreadable. She could not tell if he was calm, or just waiting to scream in her face.

Nia gulped. "Your speeches are written for you, aren't they?" she said, quietly. She winced, expecting to be struck across the face, and was surprised when the firm hand did not come.

She looked up, and the lieutenant nodded

"They are," he said. "Continue."

"And I think you remember the night when Bella and I were in the cafeteria."

"I do."

"And I think you know what we were talking about."

She watched him as he looked at her. He seemed confused by what she had said – as if he were wondering to himself whether or not she was broken. She noted her cheek was bleeding from where she had collided with the filing cabinet. A single drop of blood tickling her skin as it slid down.

"I think I do," he said.

Nia's eyes scanned the room for cameras, clocks, or wires of any kind. Eddie noted her fervent gaze.

"They can't see us, or hear us, Nia. This room is designed for storage only."

"Why should I trust you?"

"You're the one who faked a stomachache. Right now, I'm wondering whether or not I should trust *you*."

She fidgeted, uncertain. Her fingers rubbed against one another in her angst as her eyes darted about around the room, "If you knew what we were talking about, why didn't you say anything?"

"I wasn't going to accuse you of anything I wasn't certain of."

"But when it comes to Curiousness, the law states that even without concrete evidence, any potential avenue should be explored." She cleared her throat. "You failed to act. Why?"

His eyebrows dropped automatically when she said that final word. To him, a member of authority, someone who was of higher rank than Nia - he should be offended by a First Year cadet asking him questions. She was suprised to see that he was baffled. He did not respond. Nia took this to her advantage and continued:

"I think you're like me and Bella," she finally said, the words tumbling out, "I think you didn't tell anyone about the other night because you think in the same way we do. You're Curious, like us. You want out."

He thought deeply about that for a very long moment. Nia noticed how confused he looked again, as if he was struggling with something. His expression did not look encouraging nor excitable. Nia's gut sank into her boots – maybe she had misjudged him after all? She said nothing more, only gulped.

"Come to my room, tomorrow night."

Nia's throat tightened. "Your room?"

"4F in the Lieutenant's block, sixth floor."

"You want to…?" She scratched her neck and couldn't help her look of nerves. She had heard all too many rumours about those above abusing their power.

He frowned and shook his head vigorously. "No-no, I want to *talk* to you."

The look Nia gave him was still one of mistrust, so he continued: "It's nothing sinister, I promise. I simply want to have a real conversation with you, and we can't do that here, where anyone could walk in. My room doesn't have any cameras. But no one would question you being there. Maybe you could tell me what you and Bella Lockett have been planning."

Nia's eyes lit up. "So, I was right? You want out?"

He looked away for a moment, and rubbed his shoulder where it joined his neck. "I want *real*."

Nia nodded, slowly. "I need to know I can trust you."

"I promise I won't tell anybody about this, or about our meeting. You won't be ambushed."

"No, I need more than that." Nia noticed how he again was shocked by her assertiveness. She was shocked by it too. She was surprised by how he didn't respond to it, or discipline her. "I need more than just your word. I can't have you flaking out of this. If you're in, you're in for good."

He looked about the room, helpless. "What do you want from me?"

She pressed her lips together, thinking.

"Your dad is close with the Dictator, isn't he?"

Johnson nodded.

"I want his login details. For the Prohibited Web."

"Are you *mad?* I can't get hold of those. Why would he even tell me them?"

"I don't know, and I don't have to know." Nia crossed her arms. "But find them. Bring them tomorrow, when we meet. If you hand them over and they work, I'll tell you everything I know."

"You do realise that not even my mother knows that login."

"I can see why that might be the case. But you must realise that if we're going to have you as part of our team, you need to demonstrate what you can bring to the table. You need to prove you're trustworthy. And you need to prove you are worth something to us."

Nia felt her heart beating in her chest. It was like it was trying to get out. She had never spoken to anybody like that before in her whole life. Not once. And here she was, in a storage room, giving orders to her lieutenant.

"Why do you need them?"

Nia chose to tell him as little as possible. Her mind thought of the spider web scars that were stuck to Dr Schiffer's hands.

The words she had said to her on the train echoed in her ears. "There's somebody I need to get in contact with," she said, at last.

Lieutenant Johnson appeared to be thinking deeply. His jaw was set. He sniffed once and then looked up at her. He nodded, stuck out his hand.

"Deal."

Nia nodded, shook his hand, and smiled at him, "Good. I'll meet you tomorrow."

"Good," he answered. "Outside the Lieutenant Block after the evening meal. I'll have the log in. You bring whatever you think I will find interesting."

Nia nodded, and they exchanged a small smile.

"Yes, sir," she said.

"My real name's Eddie," he said, "But I cannot stress to you enough how important it is to keep up appearances here. Speak of anything like this again out in the open, and I really will have to give you a beating. And I think we would both rather that I didn't have to do that."

Before exiting the room, he had swiped his thumb gently over the blood on her cheek, cleaning her up, and made her swear to not speak of his kindness to anyone.

"If people find out about any of this, I will be forced to kill you, in front of them." His voice and gaze were stern.

Nia had nodded, knowing his words to be true. "I guess I'd have to do the same to you, too."

The smile that the two of them shared before he escorted her from the room made her whole torso tingle. His eyes were a beautiful clear blue.

Nia could think of nothing else that night. As she watched out of her window the lights in the surrounding buildings steadily turn off one by one.

She stood before the clock in her room, and watched the

hands strike 22:00, thinking so many thoughts. Most of them were of Eddie.

Bella was right all along –Lieutenant Johnson really was Curious.

And so was Nia.

CHAPTER TWENTY-THREE

67 DAYS BEFORE

He found her in the library, crying behind the History section.

"Stephanie?"

There was a sniff, followed by the sound of a crumpled up tissue being blotted against skin. Charles turned the corner, but she had her back to him.

"Are you okay?"

She turned, and her eyes were bigger than Charles had ever seen before. They were a deep chocolate brown. Her eyelashes were long and drenched with tears. It made his heart ache for her.

"You rushed off after class," he said, when she didn't reply, "I wanted to check you were alright after what happened with Mr Barker. It... it looked like he got you pretty badly."

She nodded as her bottom lip wobbled. She removed the tissue from her face, so that Charles could see. Stephanie's cheekbone was glowing from the sting. A deep bruise had already begun to appear. There was a small cut across the skin where either a fingernail or a ring had snagged her. The tissue was spattered with droplets of her blood.

"I knew he'd be angry," she eventually said. It was barely a whisper. "But I didn't expect..."

Charles nodded in agreement. "It was an overreaction. Uncalled for."

Her face upturned in sadness again as more tears squeezed out of it. She stifled a sob.

"I didn't think it would be true - the rumours. But it is, isn't it? They can do what they like to us if we break the rules."

Charles set down his bag and rummaged inside it. He brought out his own miniature first aid kit.

"Where did you get that?"

"From one of my professors. Don't worry - I'm allowed to use it. I've told the Committee of Employment Advisors I want to go into the Medical Sector. It's part of my advanced training."

She nodded and allowed him to cleanse the wound. Steadily, she seemed to be calming down and finding her words.

"It just makes me so scared, don't you agree?"

"What do you mean? Of Mr. Barker?"

"Of all of them. Of what they can do to us. Just ook at my face." She shook her head, sadly. "And this was just from forgetting to do my assignment. And I did mean to do it, I did - I was just so tired, and I fell asleep and woke up late. I figured being here on time without an assignment was better than being late and with one. Either way, I was going to get into trouble."

Charles nodded. He had some butterfly stitches and was gently placing them across Stephanie's wounded cheek. The cut was wiped clean. He could tell it stung from the way she winced and intstinvely withdrew when he initially touched her. But she trusted him. He could tell.

"What do you think they would do if we broke the big rules?" She said it in an exasperated fashion. Charles was glad when she started talking again, because he had no idea how to respond. "You know, the *important* stuff. Laws." She lowered her voice. "Curiousness."

"I... " Charles took a deep breath, looking directly at her. "I think they'd kill anybody who broke those rules."

He gave her a fresh tissue and took away the old one. She

smiled in gratitude.

"I can see why people would want to try and get out though," he said, "It's a hateful place."

"Ssh! They could be listening! Don't let people catch you saying things like that! If anybody ever asked me about it, I'd have to be truthful. I can't be killed for someone else's words."

She was visibly shaken. What had happened that day in her mathematics class would stay with her for some time. Charles was certain of it. But, he guessed, this was the result they wanted from such actions. The reason why such beatings were legal - encouraged, in fact - was to fearmonger the students into a state similar to this. Stephanie was never going to forget her assignment again. She was never going to oversleep again. And she was certainly never going to display signs of Curiousness - she was too terrified of the consequences.

And, it seemed, if anybody was to display Curiousness around her, she would report it, for fear of not coming forward with evidence. The system had worked on her.

Charles decided not to finish what he had planned on saying. He decided that Stephanie was not the person to confess his unhappy thoughts to, or ask for some level of comfort and understanding with regards to how he truly felt - how if there was a route out, he would take it. He hadn't even completed his first year at Camp Clandestine. If this was what the rest of his life was going to be like, Charles didn't know how much of it he could take.

Sure, he was scared. He didn't like the way that cadets were treated. But Charles' view was not the same as Stephanie's. He was certain.

The two of them shared a brief hug. Stephanie apeared happier for it, and deeply consoled. Charles changed the subject and agreed to help her with her mathematics assignment. She had to get it up to a high standard for Mr Barker by the end of the day. The two found a desk in the library. They sat and studied together.

They had not realised, whilst stood in the History section,

surrounded by shelves of books, that they had not been alone.

Sat on the opposite side of one of the shelving units, someone had been listening the whole time.

Dan had planned on going to console the crying girl before Charles had got there. He had stayed where he was, listening in on her words, and the underlying tones of Charles' responses. His green eyes watched them walk together out of the History section.

Silently, he gathered his books and left.

CHAPTER TWENTY-FOUR

67 DAYS BEFORE

The dining table in the Johnson's household was far larger than necessary. There were only the three of them that lived in the house. More often than not it was only the three of them that dined. It was only on the odd occassions when they entertained that there was any need for the other seating.

Regardless, they sat that evening, in their usual seats - Mr Johnson at the head of the table, his wife to his right, and Eddie to his left.

"What's wrong with you, lad? You've barely eaten anything."

Eddie looked up from his plate, meeting their gaze, if only briefly. "Nothing," he said. "Long day."

"You won't keep your strength if you don't eat your veil, darling," his mother said in her usual matter-of-fact tone. "Protein is good for you."

"Get it down you."

"I don't think I'll manage to finish the rest."

Edward Senior gave him a stern look. His lips were pressed so tightly together that they disappeared under his moustache. "I said: *get it down you*."

Eddie matched his father's gaze, but picked up his fork.

"So," his mother said, chewing delicately, "how are the new recruits?"

"Excellent. Marvellous. There's more and more of them every year - it's truly splendid, isn't it, son?"

Eddie nodded.

"I always forget how timid and mouldable they are in the first year - each of them a brand new project, just waiting to have the shyness beaten out of them. I think we're well on track for the Dictator's goals this year."

"Really? That's wonderful news! Do you think there will be enough cadets at the end of this year then? You think the numbers will stay high?"

"It's difficult to tell for sure, darling, but my hopes are certainly high. Sure, there will be a few that we have to get rid of - thin the herd, so to speak. That way we can give the strongest more of our attention. We want the strong to get stronger. We want to pummel out the weak ones as best we can."

Eddie took a heavy breath. The conversation continued for the rest of the meal. His father gloated and laughed as he spoke of how many cadets they had thrown over the wall. He told his favourite story of when a cadet hadn't been shown how to handle a gun properly and had blown his own fingers off. His father laughed until he was red in the face. Eddie stayed silent.

After the meal, his father returned to the Game Room to smoke a cigar. His mother fussed about in the kitchen, talking with the servents about how the veil was a bit too gamey. Eddie stood for a moment, suspended on the staircase, a hand on the bannister. He listened.

When he was confident they were both busy, he ascended and headed to his father's study. A quick look over his shoulder to double check - it gave him the added confidence he needed to go inside.

He sat at the desk and rifled through pages and paper and

notebooks. He was sure to put everything back precisely where he had found it.

Minutes passed and he found nothing. Eddie felt fed up. He sat down at his father's desk and heaved a great sigh. He had no idea where his father would keep his log in details for the Prohibited Web - or even if he would have them written down at all.

At a loss, Eddie picked up the newspaper that was in the bottom drawer of the desk and flicked through it. He wasn't usually one to read the paper. It was depressing.

And then he noticed the date.

In the top corner of the newspaper, like in any newspaper, there was the date of when it had been printed. This particular edition was thirteen years old.

Eddie sat forward, splaying the papers out on the desk. He scanned the pages, flicking through, looking for anything that was out of place. Was there anything scribbled in the margins, or hidden in the photographs of the articles?

Downstairs, the doorbell rang. It was closely followed by the sound of the dogs barking.

Eddie continued to search. He was being exasperated. It was here. It *had* to be here. This had to be it.

He wasn't even certain why he was so keen on looking. If anyone was to walk in at that moment and catch him snooping, things would not end well. But the thought of spending the next twenty years listening to the same stories about cadets dying made him sick to his stomach. He did not want to become his father. That would be his worst nightmare.

There was talking in the hallway downstairs. Eddie's eyes continued to scan. He had looked at every inch of the newspaper and couldn't seem to find a thing. They were just old articles, speaking of the Dictator's rise to power. They were stories he had heard a hundred times over, accompanied with adverts and the odd puzzle page...

And then he saw it.

Hidden within the completed crossword, Eddie's mind

sharply recognised an incorrect answer.

That had to be it.

He didn't have time to check it as he heard footsteps climbing the stairs. He quickly pushed up his sleeve and scribbled the username and password onto his forearm in ink. He then pushed the sleeve back down, replaced the newspaper in the drawer, and put the pen back where he had found it.

He was relieved that by the time he closed the door to the study, nobody was about to see him. He quickly made it look as if he had just come out of the bathroom.

"Eddie, dear?"

"I'm here, mother."

His mum finally turned the corner and headed along the corridor towards him.

"Ah, sweetheart, there you are. The Dictator is here, in the Game Room, with your father. They're sharing cigars. I was wondering if today was the day you'd like to meet the Dictator yourself? I'm sure they wouldn't mind you joining them in the study. After all, you will be taking over your father's role one day in the future. It could be beneficial?"

Eddie scratched his arm where the ink was drying on his skin. "I... "

His mother waited, expectently. Her lips were pursed and she blinked at him.

"As a matter of fact, I don't feel very well this evening, mother," he said, feining a grimace. "That must be why I wasn't very hungry at dinner, either. I think I'll save my first meeting with the Dictator for a day where I can make a longlasting first impression."

His mother nodded enthusiastically. "Oh, definitely! Very wise of you dear, very wise. I'll let the two of them know. Did you want anything getting for you? I can have one of the girls bring you a glass of water, or-?"

"No, no." He shook his head. "I'm just going to lie down. But thank you."

She kissed his cheek. "Feel better, dear. Do shout if you

change your mind. You do what's best for you."

He placed a hand on his bedroom door and watched her head back down the corridor. He kept his eyes on her until she had turned the corner, towards the staircase.

"I will," he said, and disappeared inside.

CHAPTER TWENTY-FIVE

67 DAYS BEFORE

Bella Lockett sat hunched at her desk in the tiny space she had been told to call home. Her bed, despite the late hour, lay untouched. Her mind, however, had never been more engaged.

She had her white binder laid out on the surface before her. A half-written essay plan lay in sight of anyone who could possibly be watching. Every now and then she would add to it. But the essay was not her main priority.

In reality it was her map she was adding to. Bella of course had already seen a map like this one, many times, in her father's slaughter shed. It was an old and tattered version from when the camps had first become a mandatory part of people's lives. Her father had taken it home with him, unsure why at the time. But, nearly twenty years later, it had finally come of some use – imprinted so vividly in the forefront of his daughter's mind. She took a red ink pen from the drawer and began to mark the map. To those oblivious, it would have seemed like she was just doodling. But to those who knew what to look for, it was a very valuable yet dangerous possession to now behold.

Bella would sit back now and then. She would close her eyes, press her lips together, gaze outside or scowl. She concentrated.

Remembered. She was using her mind's eye to the best of its ability.

A red cross here. A bigger cross there. A long, dotted line extending out from it. A bit of scribbling in.

And there it was.

Incomplete, but a wonderfully good start.

She grinned to herself as she wrote a final paragraph to her essay plan, just for show.

Bella had begun to create a document which logged every camera, every visionary clock, every spy tower throughout the campus. This included where its visionary field lay. She had known what to look out for and was now successfully beginning to fit together a large number of Red Zones to avoid in her preparations. This led to slowly uncovering small areas of white. Glistening little droplets of view-free heaven. They were few and far between, but they were there.

The Revolution was beginning.

Her father would be proud.

CHAPTER
TWENTY-SIX

66 DAYS BEFORE

I t was raining that day.

It reminded Jay of the day he and Nia were waiting for the bus. That dreary morning felt so far gone now. This new life they both had – it was so unbelievably different to the comfort of home. Everyone seemed so cold here, including his fellow cadets. Something told Jay that it was not just the rain that was draining the warmth from them.

It was Elimination Day.

"Attention!" a voice hollered, a voice whom Jay could not see the owner of. He was surrounded by many others dressed just like him. Everyone, in perfect unison, stood tall and sharp at once.

"Elimination Day," the brawly voice continued. "You lot are here because you have shown great potential. Your lieutenants have put you forth for this trial, so that you may earn greater rewards, greater responsibilities, great opportunities in the coming years here, *and* in your future. You have been chosen, as you have displayed the mark of an excellent soldier – one that the Government would be proud to be represented by in an act of war. You have shown not only physical strength, but also academic ability, punctuality, perfectionism, and an eager confidence in the trials you have faced so far. Most of all, you have shown an admirable submission, and a strength to take punishment without complaint. You should all be very proud of yourselves for standing where you do so now."

Despite the rain, Jay stood up a little taller.

"However," the gruff voice continued, "today will see just how many of you are truly eligible of the title Supreme Cadet. Before you is an assault course. It is designed to truly test your abilities as a cadet. Through these doors, you will enter in five groups, ten cadets at a time. Twenty-five of you will make it out the other side. The other twenty-five will forfeit your positions voluntarily and return to your dorms this evening in shame. Are we clear?"

In unison, a loud chorus echoed in the rain: "Yes, sir!"

"First group. Forward!"

The row of ten stepped forward. Jay watched them take their places before the entrances.

"GO!"

They sprinted into the darkness of the building. Jay felt the adrenaline begin to bubble beneath his skin. Unlike the others in his troop, he did not run or withdraw from the feeling of fear. He channelled it. He used it. That's what made him a good soldier.

A few minutes passed, then a few minutes more. Not a single sound could be heard from the building.

"Second group – forward!"

Every line stepped one pace in front. The second group of ten cadets took their places.

Jay felt his curled hair flatten down on his forehead. He squinted from the rain as another cloud broke and poured down on them all.

"GO!"

He was next.

"Third group – forward!"

They took their places. Jay prepared himself behind the line, one foot in front of the other. The grass behind the starting line was turning to thick mud with every group that disembarked.

There it was, the familiar *thump, thump, thump* of his heart. The night was beginning to close in. His stomach growled. It was 1900 hours. He had missed the evening meal. Jay hoped there would be food at the other end of the course.

His feet slipped deeper into the mud, but he held his ground. "GO!"

He ran. A slight slip, but he didn't fall, unlike a cadet to the left of him. The boy was instantly disqualified. They kicked him sharply in the stomach with a heavy boot and instructed to return to his dorm.

Jay continued to run. His black boots squelched the ground and the rain beat down upon his back. He reached his doorway and passed through the entryway to be greeted by the dark abyss of the building.

His pace slowed as he inched forward in the dark, brushing his hands along the wall as he did so, being watchful of his footing.

He inched closer and further into the nothingness.

He heard a scream.

It was a horrific sound. It steadily seemed to get further away. Then another – a male scream. He too seemed to take his fear from the neighbouring black corridor, to somewhere far, far away.

Jay began to get nervous. He had seen the faces of the others in his line. They were bold; fearless. Why did they scream?

He inched further still. His mind was confused by the darkness. He kept checking to see if his eyes really were open.

Another scream.

Jay gulped, and inched closer.

He was fairly certain that if he did not leave the tunnel before the next group entered, he would be slammed into by the next cadet and they would both instantly fail.

He lifted his foot once more and went to place it down, only to find his stomach flip at the new-found knowledge there was no more floor.

He withdrew and knelt down. Using his hands, Jay found it was the entryway to a pit. He brushed his hands along the wall. Squinting through the dark he found that the pit was no larger than four feet in diameter.

Another scream echoed in the corridor, only inches away from him, causing Jay to startle. He crouched down, thankful he had not lost his balance.

He took a gamble. He decided to jump.

How far is four feet? Well, in the daytime one may describe it as no taller than a small child, no wider than two seats pushed together, or perhaps the depth of a decent canal.

But in the dark?

In pitch black, where you cannot see your hands right in front of your face, jumping over a pit of four feet in diameter, but unknown depth, is quite a different matter.

Jay took a deep breath, as he heard the next instruction from the leader outside for the fourth group to enter. He leaped – as far as he could carry his body.

And landed.

And as his feet landed shakily on the concrete on the other side, he heard the horrific scream of a girl from right behind him.

He didn't stop to check, only continued down the dark corridor, praying his eyesight would improve.

It was only when he could see the dim light of a red bulb ahead of him that he realised – he could have warned her, he could have helped her, they could have helped each other in this.

But fear, as he found out, did strange things to people – all of them unique things, all of them individual things. But, the common theme with all of them was that they became isolated. Fear made people selfish, and cruel, and alone.

Jay felt a cold quiver shake his heart.

He shook it off and journeyed on.

CHAPTER TWENTY-SEVEN

66 DAYS BEFORE

Nia stood outside Eddie's accommodation block. The sky was grey with pollution that night. No twinkling stars could be seen in the canopy of harsh smoke. It made Nia feel only more like she was trapped inside a dome at Camp Clandestine. The outside world did not exist here. Whatever was happening outside of those stone walls would now, and possibly forever remain, a mystery.

She knocked at the front door, and almost instantly an electronic panel to the right-hand side started speaking to her.

"State your name."

"Ardenia Galloway," Nia said, somewhat uncertainly.

"Galloway, A." the automated voice buzzed. "You are not authorised to enter this building."

"I have an appointment with Lieutenant Edward Johnson."

There was a long silence. A white line appeared on the screen.

"Hello?" The line wobbled. "Lieutenant Johnson speaking."

"It's Nia."

There was a pause where nothing was said. Nia stood and waited, expecting the computer to give her further instructions. She had relied upon the knowledge of electronic equipment almost her entire life. Often, it was more reliable than a human being.

Just as she was beginning to feel unsure and wondered about leaving, the door swung open, and the Lieutenant stood behind it, barefooted and in a more casual dress than his usual green uniform.

To Nia's further surprise, he grinned.

"Come on up."

Nia stood by the door as Eddie sat down at his desk. She noted how polished and upgraded everything was in comparison to her own room. The layout was the same, the furniture was the same, but everything had that little extra *something*. It made it feel all the more rich and comforting.

The bare floorboards were covered with a thick rug, the bed was a double rather than a single. The wardrobes were set into the walls, rather than standing alone, and the bathroom appeared to have an actual bath in it. Possessions such as dressing robes, books, paintings and lampshades – they all seemed to hold a snap of personality within them. Cadets had no such luxuries. It was a larger room with not many more things inside than her own, and yet it felt so much bigger and welcoming, and warm. This room certainly *belonged* to somebody. Nia's room felt like she was merely a ghost passing through.

Eddie offered her a drink and some snacks – a choice of juices, alcohols, biscuits and dainty macaroons – all of which she politely refused. Only when instructed did she sit down on the very edge of the mattress, ever too aware of how she was crumbling the perfectly aligned bedsheets. Eddie attempted polite conversation more than once, but Nia did not engage. She was still untrusting of the lieutenant's motives.

"The macaroons are really good – made by a patisserie chef that the Dictator has under personal employm–"

"Look, let's just cut to the chase here," she said sharply. "Did you get what I asked for, or not?"

"I did."

Seeming to ignore her bluntness, he walked across the room to the grand wardrobe, opened it, and brought out a shoebox. It contained a pair of shoes so polished that Nia could see her reflexion in them on the black leather. Eddie lifted the sole of the shoe, to reveal the inside of the heel. Wound so tightly it could barely be seen, was a little scroll of paper.

He handed it to her. "It works. I've tested it."

"Well I'd like to test it for myself, thank you."

Eddie nodded, as he put everything back in the wardrobe. "There's a laptop on the desk."

She sat down in the desk chair and started up the device. The light illuminated the room and made her squint.

"You know how to load up the Prohibited Web?"

Nia cleared her throat. "I have a classmate who...knows things."

Her fingers flitted across the keys. She swiped a couple of times on the screen. A black box appeared, with a graphic of a skull in the centre.

She typed a few more keys. And then the log in appeared.

"Well, let's see how good you are to me," Nia said. It was unclear whether she was talking to the slip of paper, or to her company. She decided, intentionally, not to specify.

Eddie waited. Nia noted he looked nervous.

"Well?"

She nodded, "It works. I'm in." She quickly closed down the various web pages and tabs and shut down the computer.

"You're not going to use it now? For that person you wanted to contact?"

"I'm not going to do that with you in the room," she said, sternly. "Let's get down to business. You gave me what I wanted. What do *you* want?"

Eddie appeared to be taken aback by the question. This confused Nia, as she had presumed a man of his stature would have come prepared for a meeting such as this. She was expecting him to bring out a list of questions, points, matters of opinion.

Instead, he didn't. He sighed.

"I want to know the truth."

"Of what, exactly?"

Eddie chewed on the inside of his cheek for a second, thinking. From the desk chair in which she sat, she watched him slowly begin to pace around the room.

"Nia, I have spent my entire life, from birth until yesterday afternoon, encased in a bubble led entirely by the Government. Everything I have ever been told, everyone I have ever met, every instruction I have ever been given, has only been presented to me because someone further up the line instructed it to be so. My entire life, every day, almost every hour, is planned out for me. Every conversation has normally been implemented by another. But yesterday you stopped me by doing something unexpected. And I liked that."

He paused to let her respond, but she did not. Her gaze on him held fast and steady.

"I've never felt *right*," he said, clenching his fists above his head as he struggled to find the words. He searched for them with his eyes out of the window but was met with only the same old view as every other evening he had spent there. "I can't seem to describe it. Nothing has ever felt like it was my own, not even my decisions. I can't seem to break free from it. Whenever I think I've done something for myself, I then find out it was only presented to me because someone else decided it would be that way." Eddie noticed how Nia was looking at him.

"I don't understand where I come in," she said.

"Yes, you do," he laughed. "I know you do. I know you and Private Lockett are not up to nothing."

Nia shifted in her seat. Rather than speak, she pressed her lips more firmly together.

"My father is a powerful man. He has pulled strings and arranged meetings my entire life so I could be where I am today. For that, I am thankful. I have a life which is rich in opportunities and power and materials – but I do not feel like it's *my* life, y'know?"

"Well, I..."

"I want *in*," he said kneeling down in front of her, so they were at the same level. His eyes were bright and alive and full of wonder. He could taste the sweetness of the secrets before they had even passed his lips. "I know it's risky, and I know you have no reason to trust me, but maybe that's something we can work on." He took her hand. "But I just want to know."

Nia held his gaze in silence for a very long second, before looking down at their touching hands and pulling her own away. She cleared her throat and shifted away slightly, pulling at the collar around her neck. Her expression was unimpressed.

"This isn't safe," she finally whispered, "and I'm not even sure myself whether I want to play a part in it."

"Are you saying that because you're afraid I'm lying?"

"Would that be so bad?"

"No...I understand. I am untrustworthy. I'm the enemy that you are trying to get away from, in your eyes."

"Enemy is a strong word."

"So is ally."

They both paused for a second, equally unsure of where to go from there.

"Look, Lieutenant –"

"Eddie."

"– this is all very nice, and very tempting, but..."

"But what?" he asked. "You leave now, surely you are still in as much danger as you are if you tell me something. Right now, all I know is that there are secrets that you know you shouldn't be holding, and that would be reason enough to file a report on suspected Curious behaviour."

Nia looked at him where he knelt on the floor, pathetic and practically begging. Her eyes narrowed.

"Are you blackmailing me?"

"No," he sighed. "But listen... On the first day you arrived here, I saw Bella approach you and hand you a notelet. I saw your face. I was on guard that day, and that was behaviour I was supposed to be looking out for and reporting. But I didn't. I stood my ground, I turned a blind eye, and I let you go – that was before I even knew who you were, before I knew you were involved in any of whatever this is." He looked at her. "Does that not stand for something?"

"That was *you?*"

"Yes."

It felt so strange, this extra knowledge. Since she was a child, the world had always been presented to her in one way and one way only, and she had never questioned anything. And now, being given an alternative version of events, she realised that maybe the cause Bella was fighting for was not so helpless after all. Giving knowledge, important knowledge, to the people – that there is more than simply one way to think, and to act, and to behave – that sometimes it is okay to challenge another, and that it is okay to think for oneself, and think differently to another – to Nia, it felt like it was important.

She sighed.

"Okay," she said, "I see your point. You've given a convincing story, and you've proven you'd risk a lot to get these log-in details for me. As well as risking your personal laptop being the source of the log in, if it's documented."

His face dropped. She smiled.

"You'll be fine. I'm sure you'll be able to get rid of it somehow, or blame it on someone else. You're in a postion to do that."

Eddie exhaled heavily, most likely exhausted from the stress. He nodded. "You're right. I'll sort it."

"I'm glad we could come to a level of understanding."

He agreed, his expression very stern again. "We'll be working as a team. I understand why you needed to test me. I'll do what I can to help. So, where do we begin?"

"We begin at the end," Nia answered, with a laugh. "With our main goal. With the reason why Bella wanted to start this whole thing."

He waited for her to answer, his brows, weirdly straight, pointing into a frown.

"We're going to escape."

CHAPTER TWENTY-EIGHT

66 DAYS BEFORE

Dan had been raised in a noisy household, so he was usually a very quiet young man. Even as a lad he had kept his voice low. With five siblings of various ages, he had learned pretty quickly that he was never going to get his voice heard. He stopped trying.

However, what Dan had learned from this upbringing was the value of observing. He saw what his siblings didn't, simply because he didn't act or speak straight away. When they were all arguing about who had - or hadn't - broken something, Dan would be there already figuring out a way to fix it. Usually by the time that the argument had fizzled out, Dan had corrected the thing that had started the argument, and then disappeared out of sight. It was normally a very minor thing that they all got wound up over. Dan never got any thanks for the things he did. By the time he was a teenager, he had stopped expecting praise.

This benefitted him immensely as a soldier. Training as a cadet, Dan was able to observe a fighting move and then quickly mimic it. He was able to see a problem and quickly solve it. He was able to see the bigger picture, when others were stuck looking at it close up.

However, as the days passed by, Dan began to realise he was

seeing things that others had not. He was a great listener, a fantastic people-watcher. He could understand someone's expressions and undertones better than they could themselves.

He found himself still thinking about Stephanie and the words she had said that day in the library.

He found himself still haunted by the bloodied face of Martin as they had carried him towards the wall.

He found himself intrigued by Nia's interest in the Prohibited Web.

Somewhere, in the deepest corners of his mind, he was beginning to piece it all together. His gut was speaking to him and telling him the truth. He knew what was really going on. He could sense something bubbling under the surface. He could feel it dragging him towards it.

He was torn.

Dan was confident in his abilities, and confident that of all the cadets in the year, he was one of the elite few. He knew he could make it through Camp Clandestine, and the life beyond its walls, and excel at any duty, any problem, anything at all that they presented him with.

But was it something he wanted?

He remembered Stephanie's words and the fear she had held tightly in her voice. If Stephanie knew what Dan thought he did, she would already be reporting it to the Authorities. Nia's interest in the Prohibited Web would be squashed. Those who wanted to write home would be restricted all the more.

Was it so wrong, what Martin had been doing? Trying to speak to his parents?

Was it so bad, Charles having an opinion? Saying that he wasn't enjoying his time at the Camps?

Was it so awful, Stephanie forgetting her assignment?

Was it so horrific, Nia's interest in something that was outlawed?

And did any of these acts mean that the culprit deserved injury, or death?

Dan couldn't make his mind up just yet. But he knew which

side he was leaning towards.

One thing he did know for certain – he was going to keep his eye on Stephanie. He wasn't sure she could be trusted.

CHAPTER TWENTY-NINE

66 DAYS BEFORE

"Escape? Are you mad? There's no getting out of this place! And I work here. Belive me, I know."

"You can't help us?"

"That's not what I said." Eddie scratched his head. "What I'm saying is that I don't know how you guys are planning on doing this if I, as a lieutenant, haven't been out of this place unescorted since I first came here."

Nia sat for a long moment. "That's a shame. I was kind of hoping you'd know something that would help us."

She scrunched up her face.

"Well, I do, in a way," Eddie answered. His face was a thoughtful grimace. Just nothing to do with getting out of here. But maybe things that could help us in forming a *way* to get out of here."

"Well what do you suggest? Is there a way to get onto the train without them noticing?"

"The train?" Eddie laughed, louder than Nia thought was safe. "You really are crazy. There's no getting on that train without their permission. You saw how they board everyone didn't you? One at a time, face recognition. Seats designated with fingerprint readers. It can't be done. Nobody gets on that train without them knowing – that's how the system was designed. If we do get on, it's because they want us there. And that's *not* a position we want to be in at all. If we're where they want us, we have no power whatsoever."

"So, the best technique to go for would be… a surprise?"

He nodded. "Precisely."

Nia thought for a long moment and watched Eddie as he crouched there in front of her, excited and helpful. She realised then and there that he was not one of *them* as she had first thought. Instead, he was gentle, and he was kind. He was fiercely in favour of the cause that she and Bella were steadily working towards improving. He was not one of *them*, he was not the enemy. He was merely a young man, similar in age to herself, who wanted nothing more than to call his life his own. He wanted independence, and the freedom that would come with making his own choices and living a strong and innocent life.

"You're not all that different from us, are you?"

"What do you mean?"

"The title, the fancy bedroom, the status. It's all a show, isn't it?"

He smiled. "Yeah, I guess it is. I don't believe in any of the things they tell me to. I hate it, honestly – being a lieutenant. Makes my skin crawl."

"So when I head back this evening, I can tell Bella you're in?"

He smiled up at her with an enthusiastic nod. "Yep. I'm in."

CHAPTER THIRTY

66 DAYS BEFORE

Veronika was stood in the darkness, alone, listening to the screams of others around her as they fell. She had found safety under the light of a red bulb in the narrow corridor and was using it to catch her breath as she felt herself begin to panic.

She did not like this. She really, really did not like this.

Regardless, she knew she had to journey on. The tunnel she was in appeared to get narrower, the walls getting closer as she was drawn further into the maze. This was some sadistic joke that they liked to play on the cadets. They had said it was to test who amongst them was better than the best. To Veronika, it felt more like their eyes were watching from every direction and laughing at the ones who failed. Veronika found it incredible how many of her fellow cadets were running blindly into the darkness, only to fall such a deep and terrifying drop.

Persevere.

She took a deep breath and mustered all her courage, before starting off once more into the thick darkness. The light was so dim that it made her squint.

This challenge was more difficult in her head than it was in her body. She didn't like it. She could hear the boy in the lane next to her muttering to himself about safety and strength and needing to stay alive.

"I sympathise," she said, unknowing if she had been heard.

On the other side of the wall, Jay stopped.

"Is someone there?"

"Yeah. I've stopped for a breather. This is all messing with my head a bit."

"Same here. I'm Jay."

"I'm Veronika."

"This challenge is shit, hey?"

"Total shit. But I like a challenge," Veronika answered.

There was a chuckle.

For the first time since she had arrived, in the darkness of a dimly lit tunnel, Veronika felt she had made a friend.

CHAPTER THIRTY-ONE

66 DAYS BEFORE

Dan's least favourite part of the Elimination Day tasks was the body of water.

Icy cold. Goodness knows how deep. It was the point in the course when all the tunnels connected and Dan could see who else he was in rank with. The results did not surprise him. He could count the lot of them on his fingers - if he hadn't been swimming.

He felt he was at an advatange in this challenge. The idea of Elimination Day was to test the individual, not the group. Therefore all of the tasks were not designed to be completed within a team. Dan felt good about that. He was used to being alone – he did not think his teamwork skills would be graded as highly as he might like them to be.

Regardless, he swam as fast as he could, through the choppy dark pool. He tried his hardest not to think about what could be lurking below. He tried his hardest to believe that all cadets were taught how to swim.

They were not.

Two of the cadets he did recognise were Veronika and Jay. She had stopped at the far edge and was cheering him on. He didn't realise they were friends. He'd never seen them together before.

Veronika he had heard about on several occassions. She was a Second Year. Each year, the cadets were given a chance to keep their title of Supreme Cadet. Dan had no doubt that Veronika would do just fine. She was the strongest female cadet at the Camps, in his opinion. She could probably give a fair few of the males a run for their money, too.

Jay was a character Dan hadn't yet been able to put a firm finger on. He was determined, and a great solider, no doubt about it. But every now and again Dan thought he witnessed some fragility in Jay's stance. Was he intimidated by the fearmongering? Was he still getting used to the shock of everything, but would later adapt? It was hard to tell.

Dan looked at them inbetween coming up for breaths in the water. He was nearing the edge now, at last. He saw Veronika helping Jay out of the pool. Dan was suprised when the two of them paused.

"Give us your hand!" Jay said, leaning down towards him.

"We'll help you up!"

Without thinking, Dan reached up. They dragged him out of the water.

"You okay?" Veronika asked.

Dan nodded.

They gave him a smile and sprinted off into the darkness. The Elimination Day trials could have been leading them to the depths of hell and the pair of them practically skipped into the shadows, grinning.

Dan found himself lingering for a second, thinking about their actions. He looked down at the pool behind him, and it's choppy waters. He saw a girl struggling to get through the waves.

Dan looked at the tunnels before him. Then back at the girl.

The trials weren't meant for teamwork. The trials were about being an individual. The best solider you can be. It wasn't about anyone else. Elimination Day was selfish. The best way to ensure victory was to let those who fell behind, be left behind.

Dan knew this. He knew the way to achieve the title of Supreme Cadet. He knew that the sooner he ran down the tunnels, the sooner he would be out of the freezing cold, with a large hot dinner in front of him.

He reached down.

"Give me your hand!"

They had made it. Dan was in a room that was warm and brightly lit. The night outside had fallen. He could see it through the large windows. The sky was an inky blue, without stars. He could see the training field, and the silhouettes of a few trees.

They sat around a banquet table – the successful few, brushing elbows with the leaders of education. The lieutenants, the trainers, the Committee of Employment Advisors. Even Michelangelo Clandestine, Head of Education, was there.

Mister Clandestine made a speech. Dan didn't care to listen to it. As soon as he opened his mouth, it was clear that Michelangelo Clandestine only wanted to talk about himself and take credit for their gruelling hard work. A fire crackled and popped in a grand hearth across the other side of the dining room. Dan felt the heat beginning to return to his bones.

They had given each of them a fresh uniform. It had been hanging in their dorm rooms when they had completed the trials. The suit fit him perfectly. Its perfect craftsmenship unsettled him. He itched his neck from under the collar. Wearing a tie was uncomfortable.

When Mr Clandestine, Head of Education stopped talking, the food arrived. At long last, Dan saw exactly what his efforts had amounted to. Lamb, beef or pork – he got a choice. Honey-glazed carrots and roasted parsnips. Creamy mashed potatoes and sage and onion stuffing. Sweetened red cabbage, and buttered green beans. Copious amounts of lavish champagne. And for dessert – a vanilla and white chocolate soufflé, with raspberry gelato and caramel tuile.

"Your work was very impressive today, Veronika," Michelangelo said as he leaned in her direction. He pointed his spoon at her as he talked. "You hold great potential."

"Thank you, sir."

Dan noticed her polite, but brief response. She did not appear to enjoy having everybody's eyes on her.

"You know what is interesting to notice," he went on, "there were twenty cadets deemed worthy of the title of Supreme Cadet today. Only three of them were females. You were one of them. And – not to be rude to your fellow soldiers here tonight – but you completed the task the fastest, and to the highest ability."

Veronika's eyes shifted, uncomfortably. Dan began to eat his dessert a bit slower as he watched.

"Thank you, sir," she said again.

"*And,*" Mister Clandestine continued, pointing the spoon yet again – Dan begin to take the action as quite a rude gesture. "Do you know what that means? It means the Marital Pairings department will be *thrilled.*"

"They will?" Veronika choked on her caramel tuile. She could not hide her confusion and unease at this remark. Dan was not surprised. He had now put down his spoon, despite the soufflé being the best thing he had ever eaten.

"Certainly!" He laughed, a big white-toothed laugh. "The Supreme Cadets are always the top suitors for one another. Chances are you will be paired with someone from this very room. Having both males and females within the Supreme Cadets is a fantastic result. The Dictator is very passionate about having strong genetics remaining together. We work hard to find the absolute best male and female pairings."

Dan watched as Jay shifted uncomfortably in his seat.

"And everyone will be paired? For certain?" Veronika asked.

"They certainly will! Aren't you a lucky bunch, getting the best suitors, being matched first! After today's results they will begin the pairing analysis. Finalised results are released on your

Graduation Day, after your third and final year here is complete. You arrive here single ladies and gentlemen and leave here ready to be married and starting families of your own!"

Dan kept his eyes on the sorbet in front of him. He picked up his spoon and began to slice off another sliver of the lighter-than-air soufflé.

It appeared to Dan that Veronika wasn't keen on being matched up at all.

Dan tried to focus on crispness of the champagne as it swirled and fizzed in his mouth. Meanwhile, Michelangelo Clandestine proceeded to fill the air with the sound of his own voice, once more.

CHAPTER THIRTY-TWO

58 DAYS BEFORE

N ia stood behind the giant warehouse that was used for Elimination Day. She watched Eddie approach her across the grass. In his left hand was a large titanium briefcase. Her heartbeat quickened with excitement.

"Ready?" he asked, unlocking the back door.

"Sure am." She gave him a coy smile and led the way inside.

The room was the biggest indoor space Nia had ever seen. It was big enough to keep aircraft. Eddie informed her that, when the war eventually comes, the plan was to use the space for such things. The idea made Nia feel a disheartened.

"So," she said. "Guns."

"Yes. Guns."

He had knelt down and unclasped the briefcase. It opened to reveal several different types of handgun, encased with foam. It was cut perfectly to each weapon's shape and protected them effortlessly.

Eddie picked up one of them.

"You ever held one of these before?"

She shook her head. Shooting practice didn't begin until the second semester. This was the first time she had properly seen a gun, up close. They were due to learn how to use them after winter. But Nia and the troop didn't plan on being around that long.

"Basics parts of it: rear sight, front sight. You want to line those up when you're aiming. Magazine release–" He clicked a button, and the ammunition dropped out of the bottom of the handle. "–and this here is your magazine. Your bullets." He pointed quickly as he named the remaining parts. "Trigger, trigger guard, grip safety, slide stop, barrel, muzzle. Got it?"

She nodded, firmly.

"Alright. Let's give this a go."

He handed her the gun, and helped her to find the correct shooting position. Nia felt her body tingle as he adjusted her arms and her stance, shifting her hips slightly. His touch was gentle, his face close to her neck as he looked over her shoulder.

"Look at where you're pointing it, not at me."

"Yes. Sorry."

He mimicked the stance himself, so she could see what she looked like, and mimed holding a gun. "Point and shoot. Watch out for the recoil. That sucker will whack you in the face if you're not careful."

She nodded and took a deep breath. "What am I aiming at, exactly?"

His grin stretched across his face. "Gimme a sec."

Eddie went back to the metal case, and with a wiggle he lifted the foam out of the bottom of it. Underneath, he revealed his target.

"A laptop?"

"*My* laptop. The one you used to check the stolen login details. I still need to dipose of the evidence in case people come knocking."

Nia couldn't help but laugh.

Eddie took the laptop, opened it, and marched across the space. "Don't pull that trigger until I'm stood back behind you, okay?" He planted it on the floor, in the centre of the room, and quickly retreated.

"Ready?"

"Ready."

Nia was supringly good.

She wasn't the best – and every now and again she would through a duff shot that missed everything she was aiming at by a landslide. But given this was her first session, Eddie admitted he had had lower expectations of her abilities.

"It's actually a very good thing that you have somewhat of a natural talent for it. With less than a month before the run, you really need some sort of practice behind you."

"We'll do this every day then, if that's alright?"

He nodded. "Of course. Does Bella need lessons too?"

"No, she tells me she's been shooting since she was a kid."

"Ah, I see. Just me and you then?"

They shared a look. She smiled. "Just me and you."

CHAPTER THIRTY-THREE

32 DAYS BEFORE

Veronika and Jay, since successfully passing Elimination Day, had begun to spend a greater amount of time with one another. More than they spent with anyone else. Both had a great amount in common – their strength, their passion for exercise, their stubbornness, and their sense of humour.

"You remind me a lot of a girl I used to know," Veronika said one day. The two of them were completing an early morning lap of the camp perimeter. "She went to my school – she was beautiful. Shiniest hair you ever saw. Eyes you could swim in – and she ran just as shit as you do."

They had rare moments like this together, and their friendship seemed peculiar to those around them. A boy and a girl who enjoyed one another's company? Odd. But as the both of them were Supreme Cadets, they never hid their collaboration and their compatibility. The lieutenants thought deeply about separating them from one another – but decided against it having realised how brilliantly they encouraged other cadets to push themselves. They became, as mildly as one could be in those days, a local celebrity pairing. It led to several rumours that the Marital Pairings Department had them lined up as potential mates. Veronika and Jay both ignored these comments, as best they could.

They fulfilled their roles as Supreme Cadets remarkably well. Over the following months after the Eliminations, they acted as troop leaders in their respective groups. They delighted in slightly finer dining, slightly more comfortable bedding, and a slightly more respected presence. Veronika however remained aware of how they were being sculpted into 'Clandestine puppets'.

Veronika, Jay and their fellow Supreme Cadets were invited to join the lieutenants for a meal. They dined at the usual long, polished oak table, with multiple sets of cutlery. Hot dinners, with mashed potato free from lumps and made with real butter and seasoned with white pepper. They drank wine and felt like guests of royals. But the conversation was always returned to the same thing.

"You will all make brilliant leaders one day."

"You are not like them."

"You are better than them."

"You are one of us."

"You show potential for greatness."

Veronika watched as Jay gorged on roasted pork belly, red wine jus and asparagus. She wondered if he too had noticed the differentiation that was constantly being made between those within the room, and those in the dormitories not one block away.

It was *Them versus Us* and yet she was not sure what made the two groups different, other than the way they dressed, the way they dined, and the way they were treated. To Veronika, they were all the same.

Status was the difference. Although Veronika and Jay would never specifically be told this. Veronika and Jay had competed against others and won, and this now gave them an advantage. They were better and therefore they would be treated better. They had worked hard and so were being rewarded. Those who did not act in this way were "lesser". Those who did not know which side of a place setting that a side-plate went, or what it was used for, were beneath the men and women of power in this banquet hall. (It's the right-hand side by the way, and its usually used for bread, before a meal).

The two of them walked out of the hall at the end of the evening, tipsy from the wine. Veronika asked in a low whisper whether Jay had noticed what she had.

"Of course," Jay answered, equally quiet, "but it's like that wherever you look. It's the system they have. The rich get richer, the poor get poorer. It's an old saying isn't it?"

"I don't like it. I don't like this oppression."

"So, let's –" He hiccupped. "– let's just get out then."

"Crazy talk Jay, we're in this 'til death."

"'Til death do us part!" He laughed, but it dwindled. "Unless that's just what they want us to think."

"Huh?"

"Well what if, like, what if it's like that thing with donkeys, you know? Like they see a piece of rope in front of them and they see it as a barrier, so they never just, like, step over it and run free." He swayed as his head swirled. "Sorry – I need some water – but yeah, maybe it's like that, y'know? They put up this pretend barrier but it's not as big as everyone thinks it is. It's just the laziness of people getting in the way of their own dreams." He laughed, "But, y'know, I could be talking shit."

He shook himself a little before wandering off to his dorm. Veronika stood in the darkness of the night, watching him go. Her head began to tick with thoughts.

As stupid as he sounded, she thought, he might just be right.

CHAPTER THIRTY-FOUR

32 DAYS BEFORE

C harles was quite the opposite of Veronika and Jay in his efforts to make it through his time at the camps. Charles was not loud, nor was he boisterous. He was not the best, nor the most enthusiastic. He didn't even try the hardest. He was average. And, if he was being honest with himself, he quite liked it that way.

He did not enjoy the physical training, nor the mental training and education. His passion, above all else, was medicine.

The camp only allowed basic medical training in the first year, but Charles absorbed all that he could from the classes, and more. He spoke to his tutors about how the human body worked in greater detail. But, to Charles' surprise, his professors were more than encouraging upon hearing of this. Thus they made efforts to ensure his career path would lead to becoming a doctor.

"You will no doubt be needed in the coming years," one of his professors said to him. She sat at a large oak desk, writing a report of all that Charles had said to her. "There is always a need for medical minds, such as yours. They will soon be even more valued, no doubt, with what is to come for the country in the near future. Admirable skills such as this should never be put to waste."

She then handed him extra textbooks and medical papers, insisting that if he was to excel then he must complete all his work, plus the extra reading she was supplying for him.

"The best way to master a skill is to be ahead of all those your own age, as soon as possible," she said, "and to read, read, read! Work, work, work!"

FABLE (ADJ.)

A fictional story involving animals, most likely aimed at children, which is used to teach a valuable lesson.

Work, work, work... Everyone at the time could relate to that. I find it so odd now, looking back at the way they all used to live. It was as if it were a competition to see who could work the longest before collapsing from exhaustion; or gaining a heart condition; or turning into an entirely different person under the pressure and the stress that comes with multiple deadlines. They were working under a figurative whip, day in and day out. We can see now, of course, that this is unhealthy lifestyle. Spending every moment of every single day, doing something productive, is not compatible with the way the human brain is designed. It is the ones in charge, the ones who have the power, that keep the system this way. They crank up the pressure. They are the ones who insist on more paperwork, more deadlines, faster typing. Before the revolution it was difficult to see how this was a terrible thing. "This is just the way it is", they all said.

But I have a short fable of sorts for you. I cannot remember where exactly I found it now, but it was an experiment conducted some many years ago on apes. Six apes were kept in a large cage, in the centre of which stood a tall platform; too tall for any of the apes to see what was on top. A long rope hung down from the platform, that the apes could climb, and, unbeknownst to them, at the top, was a large pile of food.

The scientists waited to see if the apes would investigate what was on top of the platform. Being curious, they did. But, whenever any of the apes went near the rope and attempted to climb it, they were *all* sprayed with a harsh jet of icy water. Not very nice, ey?

Needless to say, none of the apes tried to climb the rope after they learned they would be punished for it.

Then, one by one, each ape was replaced with a new one, one which did not know about the icy water. The scientists noticed that when the new ape would approach the rope, the other apes would attack it, for fear of being sprayed with the water like before. But the scientists did not release a single drop from their hoses.

This happened every single time, until all the apes within the cage were new and had never experienced the icy water. All they knew was that they were not allowed to climb the rope. The pressure of their peers was too great against their curiosity, and so none of them ever tried, even though none had ever been sprayed with water, and none of them ever would be.

They didn't challenge their boundaries.

"This is just the way it is".

CHAPTER THIRTY-FIVE

30 DAYS BEFORE

N ia and Eddie met frequently. They watched the season change outside the window from the cold dreary days of winter, to the light and glinting days of spring.

Some days they would talk shooting practice. Other days they would spin problems and ideas togeher. Bella sent Nia with a list of questions each time. She said she would have asked them herself, but two of them sneaking about was far more suspicious than one. Eddie would ponder whatever she asked, and come up with answers or solutions. He was also regularly attaining supplies that Bella and Nia had requested.

In her visits, the two discussed the matter at hand, the issues they faced in everyday life, and the things they hoped for in the future. Nia talked of the possibilities of what she could do for a living, what she could learn, what she could create. She talked of a seaside cottage, on the edge of the sand. Surrounded by grassy fields and enough space and fresh air that she could carelessly walk for days with no fear of anyone or anything.

Eddie spoke of the future too, sometimes. He looked somewhat embarassed as he spoke of what he hoped for his relationships. He saw a future with a dedicated partner by his side. One whom he loved, and one whom loved him in return. *Real* love. Not elected life partners.

"All of my partners so far have always been fleeting, and nothing *real*," he said. "I think I want the real thing this time. Not like my parents have, not like anything I've had before. I want what they used to say in fairy tales. I want what they talk about in their propaganda videos about being with one and only one person. I want that."

"Pfft, he wants *you*, more like," Bella scoffed. "Do you guys actually get work done when you're over at his place? Or is there no time in between all the flirting?"

"Of course we do! Eddie has filled out the map you gave us already and corrected a few of the camera positions you placed on there. We've already begun to plan a way out of the building for each of us, as well as trying to find meeting places so we can all chat about this procedure all together."

Bella chuckled. "Oh, Nia I'm *joking*. You don't have to try and defend your innocence against me – I am not going to stand in your way, as long as we're still working towards the revolution. If anything, I think it's great you guys are hitting it off – it will add fuel to the fire, so to speak."

"What's that supposed to mean?"

"It means that you now have a real reason to help me, to get in on the cause and fight with all your might." She raised an eyebrow.

"But we're not together or anything."

"Exactly. But if any part of you really *wanted* to be, no member of the Government would approve of that. He's military, he's prestige. You come from the most common of common families there are, with a father branded as Curious. You have nothing towards your name that the Government or Eddie's parents would class as exceptional. You're boring. On record, you are probably far from a designated match for one another. They wouldn't allow it."

"Well why not? That's just ridiculous!"

"I know," Bella answered, matter-of-factly. "The whole pairing-up system is a load of bollocks. *Some* of us ladies don't want to be paired with men – the choice would be nice, y'know? Anyway, my point is – the heated response you have to the scenario tells me one thing. You're against it all, too. And you are not someone who is against something for no reason, Nia. You *like* him."

"I..."

"It's okay, little chicken," Bella said, "I'll make sure they don't kill you for being who you are. But for goodness sake, our time here could be short, and you guys need to face the reality that we might not make it over the other side of that wall."

"So, what are you saying?"

"I'm saying that if I had a guy or gal who fancied me, I'd never leave their bedroom. Speak to Eddie, and do it as soon as you can," she said. "This life is too short and too bitter to be scared of a little rejection."

CHAPTER THIRTY-SIX

30 DAYS BEFORE

K*nock-knock-knock-knock-knock-knock-knock-knock.*

It was ceaseless. Nia and Bella looked up from their work and at Bella's bedroom door. They dared not speak. Both of their hearts skipped several beats.

"It's okay," Bella whispered, without moving her lips. "It's probably nothing."

She got up from her desk and straightened her clothes. Nia did her best and covered the illegal papers with homework they had also been completing.

Knock-knock-knock-knock-knock

"Coming!"

For the first time since the two had met, Bella was visibly nervous. It was subtler than considered average, but there was undoubtedly a shake to her voice, a quake to her hand, and a rigidity with which she moved.

Bella unlocked the door. She wsa faced by a girl she vaguely recognised but had never spoken to directly. Warm-brown skin and jet-black braided hair, that was incredibly shiny, if a little strewn. She was strong and stood tall, with broad shoulders. She was in the year above Bella and Ardenia. And, if Bella was not mistaken, she was a Supreme Cadet.

"Is Nia Galloway here?" she asked, feverishly. Her eyes were wide.

Bella paused for a second, before stepping to one side and allowing the girl to enter. Behind her stood a tall, strong young man with curly dark blonde hair. He too looked equally as eager, and equally as unsure.

"Jay?" Nia stood up. Everyone in the room looked between one another.

"Come with us," Bella said. "People might be listening from the neighbouring rooms. I know a place nearby where we can talk."

It was the cupboard under the stairwell, two floors down. A bit of a squish with the four of them. Surrounded by cobwebs and old picture frames and spare moth-bitten bed sheets, they found a sense of security.

"Jay and I became Supreme Cadets after surviving Elimination Day," Veronika Shaw explained, "but since then, I think we've both being challenging the way things are run, and the expectations that those above have of us. Jay mentioned how Nia had experienced doubts upon first arriving here, and about the doctor who conducted her medical examination."

"Doctor Schiffer, yes."

"Do you know where she is now?"

Nia shifted uncomfortably and batted away a cobweb in her line of sight. "No, I didn't see her again after the train journey. I tried contacting her but got no reply. I'm still trying, though. I can only presume she went back to the city."

Correct.

"She's probably working in a hospital or something now and has forgotten anything she said to me."

Wrong.

"That's a possibility," Bella added. "But... speaking the way she did in front of new cadets – that's incredibly risky business.

Curious Talk, treason, all the bad things the Government don't want to come out of people's mouths, particularly people of influence, like a doctor. I wouldn't say she is very safe."

She's dead, guys. She's already dead.

"Neither are we, stood in a cupboard chatting shit about a revolution," Veronika said, followed by a long and awkward silence.

> They were daring kids – but they were still just kids, really. Each of them was there that day because they were willing to risk everything. But each of them was still equally scared. Like I said before, death is a cruel and sinister being, ever-present and doubly gruesome back then, too. The exposure that each of them had experienced to death so far in their short lives was diverse but made none of them less scared than the other. Each of them still had something to lose.

"So, what's the plan you guys got so far?" Jay asked. His words broke the uneasiness of the group, and Bella eagerly brought out the well-worn map from her pocket.

"This map contains the locations of each of the security cameras and watchtowers. It also marks where things like barbed wire line the fences, which fences are climbable, where the residential blocks for the soldiers lie, all that kind of stuff."

"Whoa..." Veronika took it from Bella and admired her handiwork. "This is nice. How'd you manage to do this?"

"It's nowhere near finished yet," Bella said and tugged it back, "but from this, we should be able to figure out an escape route."

"It's suicide," Jay said.

"No, it's risky. But it's possible. We've got one of the lieutenants in on it too."

"Holy shit, really?"

"Lieutenant Johnson," Nia explained, "he wants out."

"Of the system?"

"Of everything. They're just as controlling to the soldiers as they are to the cadets, the civilians."

"Yeah, we found that too," Veronika said, nudging Jay. "They just bribe them for their loyalty with food and booze, mostly."

"Nia's been speaking with him in private in the evenings," Bella explained. She folded the map back into her pocket. "Sharing ideas with him, and seeing if he knows anything that could help us."

Nia nodded. "He has access to places we don't. We're trying to work out if he can shut off the power that evening for us or not. It'll be tricky, but it will mean all the cameras would be out. He's also been teaching me how to shoot, so might be able to get us access to supplies. Knives, guns, ammo, that kind of thing."

"Ammo? We're gonna massacre the place?" Veronika and Jay visibly withdrew in the tiny space of the cupboard.

"That's not the plan." Bella shook her head. "But if it comes to it, we might have to shoot someone. Or, a few people." She saw their uneasy expressions. "That's alright with you guys, right?"

Jay cleared his throat. "I wouldn't say I'm alright with it. But, if it's the only option–"

"It might be."

"Then yeah, I'm cool with that."

"Does this mean we're all on board?"

There was a quiet chorus of agreement. Their tiny band had grown to a steady group of five.

The revolution was beginning. In a way, the Dictator was right. Curiousness really did spread fast.

THRALL (N.)

The state of being under great influence of somebody's power.

Although this story is filled with individuals who were not blinded by the rules and brainwashing, I am sad to say that, for the majority, this was not the case.

The case of Stephanie Brownlee was, sadly, a standard one.

The lessons, the laws, the idea of Curiousness as a disease... Stephanie fell for it all. She had always been of a weaker mind than the founders of the Rebellion. But it was being struck across the face - feeling that very real pain, that very real consequence - which pushed her over the edge.

It had not been coincidental that she found herself outside the broom cupboard on the same day as the others. Stephanie had been given a dorm room on the same floor as Bella's from day one of the semester. She had always wondered where she disappeared off to, on such a regular occurrence. She wondered why her and Ardenia were so often spending time together. At first, Stephanie had presumed it was something romantic. With all pairings being forbidden by law other than approved male and female matches, Stephanie did not like what she was seeing.

She was correct about something not being quite right but was wrong about the subject matter. But it was on this day that Stephanie decided to follow the group of four down the corridor, to see what was going on.

Unbeknown to the group, she stood outside and listened. She was appalled by what she heard, and it filled her with fear. She was now just as guilty as they were, harbouring this knowledge. The consequences scared her.

And, unbeknownst the Stephanie, as she observed something she was not supposed to, another set of eyes were present in the corridor.

He didn't plan it. He was just there. The lift doors opened, and Dan saw Stephanie, pale as a sheet.

He asked her if she was okay.

She shook her head no. And then changed her mind and nodded instead.

Stephanie scurried off down the corridor, and Dan watched her go.

He was good at observing. He wasn't quite sure how he felt about what he had just witnessed.

But he made a mental note to keep a closer eye on Stephanie.

CHAPTER THIRTY-SEVEN

28 DAYS BEFORE

Nia shoved her hands into her pockets. Nights like this were bitterly cold. She hurried her pace as she crossed the campus, looking forward to the warmth of Eddie's dormroom.

He was stood at the entrance when she arrived. She saw his silhouette leaning in the doorframe and couldn't help but smile. She alternated the nights between Bella and Eddie, to ensure everybody was kept in the loop. But she had to admit, the ones where she was meeting Eddie always made her a more excited.

He stepped aside as she approached, so she could enter. The warmth of the building smacked her in the face, and she loved it.

"We need two more handguns."

"Two?" He pressed the button to call the lift.

"At least."

"What for?"

Nia rubbed her hands together as the doors to the lift opened. They got in.

"Two new recruits. My cousin, Jay, and his friend Veronika."

Eddie frowned. "Do they, er... do they need shooting practice, too?"

She shook her head. "Supreme Cadets. Accelerated training programme."

He relaxed.

"Don't worry," she said, coyly. "Nobody's going to be storming in on your private tutoring."

She shoved him playfully, and the doors to the lift opened. They instinctively lowered their voices as they walked down the corridor.

"They any good?"

"Very good. Veronika is supposed to be the best cadet in her year. They have high hopes for her."

"What about Jay?"

They turned the corner.

"Well, he's–"

"Father?" Eddie said, as he elbowed Nia sharply in the ribs.

"Ah, here you are," Edward Senior said. "I've been knocking at your door. Where have you been?"

"I was..." Eddie glanced briefly at Nia. Both of them had wide eyes.

"Who's this?"

"Erm–"

"Galloway, sir." Nia bowed her head. "A pleasure to meet you."

Edward Senior noted the stripes on her uniform. "You're a First Year. What are you doing in the Lieutenant Block?"

"She was–" Eddie began.

"I'm providing a service for Lieutenant Johnson, sir." Nia said. She kept her eyes downwards.

"Service, ey?"

The pair nodded.

Edward Senior looked down his nose at Nia. She was sure to keep her eyes on the ground.

"Very well then," he said. "I'll leave you to your business. But come and speak to me afterwards, Edward. I need to ask you about the Marital Pairing system. Your results will be presented this year. I want to run a few things by you."

Eddie nodded. "Sure."

Edward Senior walked back down the corridor and headed towards the lift. Nia noticed he limped heavily on his left leg. Eddie opened the door to his room and led them inside.

"Quick thinking on your part," he said. "Thanks for that. I didn't realise he'd be here."

"No matter." Nia shrugged.

Eddie fussed about getting his notepapers from where they were hidden under a floorboard. Nia kept her eyes on him.

"Marital Pairings, huh?"

Eddie looked up. "Yeah, he wishes."

"How did he get his limp?"

"Attacked by a scent hound. They did a search but gave him the wrong parameters. He walked right through the dog's scent path and it snagged him. Ripped his leg to shreds. Wasn't that long ago. The doctor didn't do a bad job patching him back up again, though."

Nia sat down on the bed and thought of Doctor Schiffer. She had managed to covertly send a few extensions of contact with the login details, but had heard nothing back. Nia was beginning to think that she needed another angle. The problem was, she couldn't think of any other means of reaching her.

"I still haven't managed to contact that person," she said.

"Who?"

"The one I wanted the login details for. The doctor."

"Does it not say their location on their file?"

"What do you mean?"

"The Prohibited Web is also used for the Governmental Files. Everybody's infomation is on there – including their last known location. You should be able to search her, find her home address. Maybe we can find a way to smuggle a letter to her."

She beamed. "Eddie, you're a genius!"

"Well..."

"Where's your laptop?"

"In the bin. You shot it to pieces, remember?"

"Fuck... Of course I did." She rubbed her forhead as she thought. "You don't have a replacement?"

"Not yet, no."

"Don't worry," she said, confidently. "I'll think of something."

CHAPTER THIRTY-EIGHT

25 DAYS BEFORE

"Right..." Dan looked uneasy. "So, what is it you're doing exactly?"

"The less you know, the better," Nia told him, loading up the computer. "Just keep watch, okay?"

She watched him hesitate, teetering on his toes as he struggled with it in his mind.

"I just don't know how I feel about-"

"Ssh. I'll be quick. I promise."

Nia kicked off her left boot, whipping off the sock with her thumb in one quick movement. She removed the piece of paper that was tucked discreetly between her toes, before putting her shoe back on again – in case a quick getaway was needed.

She loaded up the web browser and her fingers danced across the keys. Then, a few more clicks and buttons, and she was where she wanted to be.

The Prohibited Web.

The screen was all inverted. The writing was white, on a background of black. The login box waited patiently, the cursor blinking at her.

"I'm a bit confused as to why this needed to be done *now*-"

"Ssh. Keep your voice down. Please."

Nia had originally planned for Bella to keep watch for her, but she was out on a discplinary jog. Bella's classmate hadn't had enough team spirit that day, according to their lieutenant. Nia was still trying to decide whether asking Dan to step in was a good idea or not. So far it was proving to be more effort than she needed it to be.

She gently uncurled the little piece of paper. It wasn't even as long as her index finger. In neat letters, written in fountain pen she read:

Log In: EJohnson4
Password: B_xlt4yP

"What's that?"

Her hand instinctively curled around the piece of paper as Dan made himself known behind her. It unsettled her how quietly he could move.

"Nothing." She hit the enter key and the screen loaded.

"You're on the *Prohibited Web*?"

"Will you *please* go and stand by the door, like we agreed?"

Dan cleared his throat, evidently uncomfortable.

"Dan, all I'm asking of you is that you tell me if somebody's coming. I'm doing five of your assignments in exchange for this. You don't need to know what I'm up to. It's better for you if you don't. The more you know, the more invested you are in this. And believe me, there's no way to back out." She was staring at him, her expression stern. *"Please.* Go and keep watch for me."

He nodded, thoughtful, and did as instructed.

"You can trust me, you know," he said.

There was only the light of the computer monitor, and the sound of Nia's typing. She paused.

"Maybe," she said.

The search bar was illuminated before her. She'd managed to find the database she was looking for. The files. The Governmental files. Nia had never imagined she would ever be doing something as unlawful as this. Only those with designated access were allowed to read the files - Nia didn't even have full access to her *own* file. What she was doing was incredibly risky. If she was discovered, she would not be taken away. She would be shot.

She hovered the cursor over the search bar, clicked, and began to type:

Suzanne Schiffer.

There were thousands of entries, from all over the country. Nia had to refine the search by occupation in order to whittle it down.

There she was. Her pale, timid face glowed at her through the screen.

Nia pressed her lips together, knowing there was no turning back if she opened it.

She was really doing this. She was starting a revolution. She was becoming a felon.

Nia opened the file.

"Oh my gosh..."

Her mouth dropped open involuntarily. She couldn't stop blinking. The words glowed back at her.

"What?" Dan asked, from by the door. "What's wrong?"

When Nia didn't answer, he came over to her. She couldn't speak to tell him not to look.

"Hey, that's one of the doctors from the train, isn't it?"

Nia nodded. "I've been trying to contact her. There's been no response. I needed to sneak back on here in order to check her files. To check..."

Her voice drifted off.

Dan leaned over her shoulder to get a better look at the screen. He was the type where his lips would move when he read something. Nia could hear him mumbling under his breath.

"Shit..." he eventually said.

They both stared at the screen. Nia had stopped caring whether Dan knew or not what she was up to. She knew he wasn't an idiot - he could figure this out if he tried hard enough. It was just a risk she was going to have to take. Her brain was in too much shock to tell him to back away from the screen.

The words stared back at her, blazing white against the dark background:

Name: Suzanne Sigourney Schiffer.
Sector: Medical.
Occupation: Doctor.
Age: 34 years.
Deceased: 107 days.
Cause of Death: Authority Approved Disposal.
Disposal Method: Strangulation.

There it was, clear as anything. In writing. Doctor Schiffer would be of no help to Nia, Bella or their mission. The Government had made sure of that.

"Did you know her?"

"Not really."

Dan drummed his fingers against the desk, thinking. He stood up straight again.

"You see what it said there, about her scars? *Electrocution?*"

Nia nodded, slowly. "I saw."

Dan ran his hands through his hair and shook his head. "I might not want to know the answer to this," he prefaced, "but I have to ask. Why did you need to access the Prohibited Web? And why are you searching Government files to find out about this woman?"

Nia felt dread seeping into her toes. She chose her words carefully.

"Dan," she said, "if you have to ask, then you wouldn't understand."

She began to log out of the computer, turning everything off, removing any trace of herself that she had been there. She tucked the slip of paper into the elasticated waistband of her underwear.

"You said I can trust you," she said, standing up so they were eye to eye with each other. "You meant that, right?"

He nodded.

"Good. Please don't tell anybody about this. Because if you do, I'll kill you before anybody else has a chance to. I mean that."

Her voice was calm, collected. She wasn't making a threat. Just stating a fact. She would have no other choice. There was more at stake here than just her own life.

"I understand." He nodded. "You have my word."

CHAPTER THIRTY-NINE

20 DAYS BEFORE

It had been Nia who had asked for shooting practice, being the forward-thinking girl that she was. Eddie had readily agreed to it.

The pair had spent a fair few evenings in the empty warehouse, working on Nia's aim. Whenever they had a few hours to spare when they could disappear off together, they would make the most of it. There was an electricity to the air that Nia found addictive. She couldn't quite work out whether it was the idea of getting caught learning how to shoot, or whether it was her company. She was beginning to think it was the latter.

Nia finished shooting her round. Eddie had smuggled some paper targets for her to aim at. With each session, the center of the target was torn through more and more. By this point, they were in tatters.

"When did you learn to shoot?" Nia asked. She dropped the magazine out of the gun. Eddie handed her a fresh one.

"When I was a kid. Way before I came here."

"How old?"

"I don't remember. Eight? My father forced me to shoot our cat."

Nia grimaced. "Really?"

"Yeah, he always hated it. My mother wasn't especially happy when she heard the news."

"I can understand why."

Eddie dug his thumbnail into the skin on his hand. He cleared his throat.

"So he's always been like that?" Nia put the safety on the gun and crouched down next to him.

"Ha, what do you think?"

"I imagine people are born nobheads."

Eddie laughed. "That's one way to put it." He scratched his head. "My father likes to push people. Always has. I'm one of his favourite people to push."

"Is that why you're the youngest lieutenant here?"

"The youngest ever, yeah. He told me it would happen even before I started my initial cadet training. Put me on an express pass through everything."

"I bet that was intense."

"It was... and I'm not ungrateful. I know a lot of people would kill for the opportunities and the upbringing I was given. But, for me, it wasn't what I wanted. I know this place isn't exactly designed for making friends, but I had none. Everybody was scared of me because they knew who my father was."

"They didn't want to talk to you?"

Eddie grimaced. "It's lonely at the top."

They both looked at the floor.

"Well, you don't look half bad for it. He may have made you work hard, but you've come out better. If it weren't for your training and abilities, you'd be of no use to me."

He looked at her and she winked.

"Now stop trying to make me give you pity for your lonely life of luxury. We've got work to do."

It was on the walk back across the grass when it began to rain. The clouds had been drizzling pathetically all day, but that evening they had eventually given up and unleashed a downpour so strong that the droplets stung when they hit their faces. It was the type of downpour where it was no use even trying to pull your jacket up over your head. The rain would soak them through, no matter what. Nia and Eddie found themselves laughing – they couldn't help it.

They tried to take shelter under one of the few trees on the campus, but its branches were sparse and they still were not completely dry. The pair had sprinted, hoping for shelter, but laughed even harder when they discovered it was no use. It was ridiculous, really. They were drenched to the skin.

Nia looked over at Eddie and found she enjoyed the look on his face. She hadn't seen a true smile on him. She had forgotten herself what it felt like to laugh – *really* laugh. It made her muscles ache, it had been that long. Eddie's eyes lit up, rainwater dripping from his eyebrows and hair. The rain brought with it a crisp, fresh air that they breathed deeply into their lungs. In the darkness of the night, with only the pair of them about, it felt magical.

The laughter died down. Nia had Bella's words echoing around her head.

This life is too short and too bitter to be scared of a little rejection.

Nia thought of how Doctor Schiffer had told her to run, how she had been killed for telling her so. Nia thought about the fear and the hatred, and the deaths she had witnessed since she arrived. She thought about the way that the Dictator and the Government wanted her to live, and how having those huge choices ripped away from her made her angry. She thought about Eddie's smile, and his laugh, and his blue eyes – and how it made her heart beat faster, and her fingertips tingle. And how all she wanted to do was be closer to him, and to see what happened.

She stepped towads him, in the rain. Her face held a look of curiosity and assertiveness that she'd never had before.

Nia wasn't going to let them take away her freedom, her right to choose. She wasn't going to let them keep here here, within these walls, answering to their every whim. She wasn't going to let them choose her job, her husband, her life. She wanted those choices for herself. For once, she wasn't going to wait to be told what to do.

Nia placed herself in front of him. She watched his eyes flicker in confusion. The silence that followed lasted only a second but was the longest moment that Nia could ever comprehend when she looked back on it in years to come. The moment where his lips were just an inch or so from her own. She wrapped a hand upwards from his chest, around his neck, his shoulder. It felt like everything was going in slow-motion, as she pulled him closer, and their lips touched delicately. He didn't draw away.

"Eddie," she said, reaching for his hand, "let's go back to your room."

It happened again, and again. By the time they reached the lieutenants accomodation block, the two of them couldn't get the doors open fast enough. She wanted to press her lips against every inch of him. She wanted to feel something that she *wanted* to feel. This wasn't something that had been approved by anyone, she hadn't reached a certain phase in her education to say that she was adequately prepared. She was just ready. She had made this decision by herself. They had made it together. It was liberating.

"I didn't plan on–" Eddie said.

She kissed him to quieten his thought. "I know. I didn't either."

"This is–"

"Good?"

"*Yeah.*"

She pushed him back on the bed and kissed his neck, pressing herself against him. The world sped up from that moment on. It was a sensation that Nia and Eddie had never felt before – neither alone nor together. The feeling that you associated with being absorbed in a brilliant song and allowing your body to move and to dance however it wanted to. Unaware of time or others. Absorbed, captured, engaged entirely with just the moment and the sensations in the seconds as they came and went.

With just a single light in the room to light the way, and nothing but their hearts to set the rhythm of the beat, as fast-paced as they were. They had both allowed themselves to have what they wanted. They had both allowed themselves to not think of the consequence, or even if there was one. They did not have moments where they even wanted to think. They were together in the darkness, their clothes falling to the floor, their bodies intertwined and sharing the warmth of their skin with one another.

They tumbled together on the bed sheets, consumed by pleasure.

There were no forms to fill out, no processes, no rules, no procedures. It was a freefall.

There may have been trouble ahead, cold days, and colder nights - lengths at a time when they would be running as fast as they could in order to survive, to stay together, to fight for their freedom and their right to be with one another. But as they began to fall so innocently in love, they were not concerned with any of that.

Afterwards, they lay wrapped in one another's arms, collapsed on the floor, hearts steadily climbing down from their magnificent high. Nia felt the tickle of Eddie's fingertips as they ran through her long hair, and caressed the outline of her body, his eyelashes fluttering against her cheek whenever he blinked. He touched her so gently, with such care, such mindfulness, that it gave her goosebumps all over. He pulled her closer, inhaling her. Neither of them could believe where they were, what had happened, how it had happened. So suddenly, so unexpected, so forbidden. But so perfect, and so right.

They had spent their lives trying to find a haven, a place to call safe, a place to have confidence enough to make their own choices.

In each other, they had finally discovered it.

CHAPTER FORTY

19 DAYS BEFORE

Charles walked hurriedly through the hallway, clutching his medical books to his chest and muttering to himself over and over all the things he had to do that evening, and in what order they had to be done. With each quickened step, he tapped a finger against the hardback cover of one of the books closest to his gripping hands, counting off what he needed to do. This repetition, he found, made it easier to remember something before he had a chance to write it down.

His head was down, his pace was fast, his mind was far away.

THWACK.

Charles ran into someone who was in an equally distracted state.

"I'm sorry, I'm so sorry!" he said, suddenly alert, as he watched his books clatter to the ground, the heaviest of which appeared to have landed on the other person's foot.

"Fuck! No, it's fine, honestly – I'm fine! I should have been looking where I was going. Hey – it's Charles, isn't it?"

He looked up, and to his surprise, recognised the friendly face smiling back at him. They had sat opposite one another on the first day in the dining hall and shared rumours about what was to come for them both.

"Nia!" He felt as if he could hug her, but he wasn't exactly sure why. "How're things?"

"Not bad thanks, not bad." They began collecting the books

together. "What about you? I don't remember seeing this book on the curriculum. Are you taking an extra course?" Nia looked down at the dull old covers of the medical books that littered the local vicinity. Charles felt a twinge of sadness in his heart.

"Yes, in a way," he sighed. "It's a lot of hard work, but it's something I really want to do."

"Medicine?"

"I want to be a doctor. And my professor says I have very high potential, so I need to start absorbing as much of this information as I can now, so that when my cadet training is over I can continue a career as a doctor for the army."

"For the army?"

"Yeah, my professor said that's what I should be doing, and that more positions will open up soon. Apparently there's a war coming or something."

Nia smirked. "Yeah, apparently there is."

"Where are you off to?"

"Um, nowhere. Just a friend's dorm. We have a small study group in the evening." She handed Charles the other half of his stack of books. "Good luck with your medical training."

She hurried off down the corridor, disappearing into a dorm room with a smile in Charles' direction.

He was left feeling dazed, and very much intrigued by Nia.

His professors were not wrong. Charles Vanderbilt was indeed a very smart young man.

CHAPTER FORTY-ONE

19 DAYS BEFORE

G iven what he had witnessed in the previous weeks, Dan's brain was filled with various words, imagery and thoughts.

Martin's dead body, being slung over the wall.

The face of Doctor Schiffer on the Prohibited Web.

Stephanie's pasty form as she ran away from the broom cupboard.

Daniel sometimes felt that being as observant as he was could be more of a curse than a blessing. His brain would pick out things that other people just wouldn't see. It would demand that he pay attention to them, to piece the puzzle together. Normally, it would be manageable, easy struggles. But lately, the things he had been confronted with were all-consuming.

Dan had a feeling he knew what the subject matter was about. He had a feeling that Curiousness was involved. But he had sworn to Nia that he could be trusted. Whatever she was up to did not concern him. He wasn't interested - he was going to stay out of it.

That was going to be the case, at least, until Dan saw Stephanie quick-marching her way to the entrance hall of the main building.

Her face was stricken with unease. Dan recognised her immediately and found himself jogging to catch up with her.

"Hey," he said, and then, "*Hey!*" when she still didn't stop.

He touched her arm. Stephanie halted and spun around. Her eyes were wide, like always. For some reason she always looked on the verge of tears.

"What's wrong?"

She shook her head. "Nothing."

"It's clearly something."

"I *don't* want to talk about it."

Dan went quiet, respecting her wish, but found that she didn't make a move to continue on her way, like he thought she would.

"You look like you're in a rush to get somewhere."

"I was heading to the main building."

"You have an appointment?"

"No." She paused, clearly having not thought about that issue, "But they would listen to me. They'd let me in. They'd want to hear what I have to say."

Her eyes flickered about, trying to tell if anybody else was listening in on them. Dan did the same. He took her elbow and led her around a corner, underneath a fire escape. From here, passers-by would not be able to see them.

"What's this about?" Dan pressed. "I saw you the other day when I came out of the lift. You looked shaken then, too. Something's bothering you."

"I... " Her eyes darted about again. She kept interlinking her fingers in different ways and then untangling them. Her eyes looked glassy again, pricked with tears.

Dan didn't let his green eyes look anywhere else but at her. She had his full attention. "You can trust me, you know," he said.

Stephanie took a deep breath, calming herself. "Okay," she said, "you're right. I do have something on my mind. But it's big. And it's scary. And I need to tell somebody right away and report it."

"What is it? You can tell me."

"It's... " She looked about her again. Then she leaned in closer to him and lowered her voice. "It's Curiousness...it's here. In the

Camps."

"You're not serious?"

She nodded vigorously. "I am. It's true."

"Where? Who?"

"There's four of them. Bella Locket. Ardenia Galloway. They're the big two. But there's two more, two Supreme Cadets. Veronika Shaw and Jay... Jay something."

"I know who you mean. Jay Galloway. They're related."

"Siblings?"

"Cousins."

She snapped her fingers. "So it *is* to do with genetics."

Dan watched her flit about with her hands. She was fidgeting. She was eager. She kept looking at the entrance to the main building, over her shoulder.

"Listen, um..." Dan began, bringing her gaze back onto him, "you still seem a bit shaken up. How about we sit down somewhere for a bit and talk this out, so you're not so scared about it? You can tell me everything. And then we can go and report it together. How does that sound?"

Stephanie's wide eyes gazed at him, adoringly. "Really? You'd come with me?"

"Yes, of course I would... I just need to understand better, first. Is that okay?"

She nodded and smiled.

"Cool, I know somewhere we can go."

He took her by the elbow again and led her towards the field. It stretched for miles, but he knew where to go. Dan had noticed it when he had completed Elimination Day. There was a spot behind the edge of the warehouse. He took her there. She struggled to keep up with his pace.

When they got there, he didn't give her a chance to speak. He changed his gentle grip on her elbow and twisted her around to face him. Then, he swept a leg at her ankles, knocking her to the ground.

"Stop! Ple-!"

He grappled her. He pinned her to the ground. He clenched

his fists and he struck her across the face repeatedly. Her nose was the first to bust open, gushing blood all over her face and his hands. Bruises swelled up under her eyesockets - and then he felt one of them break. He didn't aim his swings. He just struck as hard, and as fast as he can. He tried to make the blows fast and effective.

Every time he struck, he thought it would be the last time. He thought she would stop making noises, cries, pleas, gargles as she choked on her own blood. Each time, he was mistaken.

He had wanted to use his gun. He had wanted to make it quick and painless. But unauthorised gun use was forbidden. He couldn't risk someone investigating the crime as it was taking place.

Eventually, he felt her go limp. She stopped fighting him. The lights faded from her eyes and he allowed himself to stop and catch his breath.

Without hesitation, without thinking, he climbed off her, and hauled her body over his shoulders. He walked across the field with her in his arms. He knew that, given it was such a regular occurrence, nobody would stop and ask him why he was carrying a body across the field. Given she was not the strongest, nor the smartest, they would not put in the effort and resources needed to discover why she had disappeared.

Dan reached the nearest wall and attempted to throw her over. He was unsuccessful. A fellow cadet saw him struggling and came to assist.

"What happened?" he asked.

"She was asking for it." The words fell out of his mouth. They didn't sound like his own.

The cadet laughed and helped him push her over the wall. They both wiped their hands on their trousers. Dan thanked him. They went their separate ways.

Dan walked back to his dorm room on autopilot. His hands were covered in blood that was not his own.

He scratched Stephanie's name off the list on her floor.

He walked up the stairs.

He sat down on his bed and stared at his hands.

Then burst into tears, ashamed of the monster he had become.

CHAPTER FORTY-TWO

19 DAYS BEFORE

Nia slid into Bella's room. She was hunched over at her desk, completing the day's coursework before their session officially began.

"Is it safe?"

"Yeah," Bella said absent-mindedly, "I've covered the microphone today with my coat, so if we speak in a quiet voice, we should be fine." She punched an aggressive full-stop at the end of her last sentence, before setting down the pen. "The camera is back up though, so don't act suspicious." She laughed.

Nia collapsed onto the bed in exhaustion. The physical training that day had been especially rough. They had waded through thigh-high mud, been forced to swim in icy waters, and had their lung capacity tested time and again to see how long they could stay underneath the surface. Nia's eyes felt swollen. Her legs and arms were covered in bruises from the fist-fighting practice, and her bones still felt chill from the temperatures they had been exposed to. She had a yearning to simply curl up in her bed and embrace the darkness and quiet that came with restful sleep.

But, of course, the night did not end yet. There was still work to do.

"So, how is Eddie?"

Nia blushed and straightened her hair. "He's good."

Bella's eyes slid over to her suspiciously. Her lips carried a small smirk.

"He's good, is he?"

"Mm hmm."

"How did your talk go?"

"Well. It went well." She sat up again on the bed and shrugged her shoulders. "He likes me too."

She felt awfully shy. She could tell that Bella knew something else had gone on.

"I'm not going to pry." Bella laughed, and winked at her. "But I think a little more than talking happened between you two… am I right?"

Nia couldn't control her grin. "Shut up," she said, "we need to get work done."

Nia did eventually spill the beans to Bella and thanked her sincerely for her help in getting the two of them to confront their feelings. She strongly believed in using your words to solve problems, as well as avoid them. Everything just seemed a lot simpler to her if people expressed how they felt freely, calmly, and without judgement. So many problems could be avoided, and so many couples could get together (or get over one another) much sooner.

I have to say I agree with her on this one, too. Imagine if the advisors of the Dictator had just all sat down together in the same room and gone "Look, what is it you're actually planning here? Will you tell us? Cause we'd all really like to know." And when the Dictator explained the vision for ultimate power, control and manipulation of the country, and eventually the entire of the human race, all the advisors would have brought it up with a medical professional, the Dictator would have been sent away to a padded room, and the whole political situation could have been avoided.

It was the early hours of the morning before Bella suggested the idea of turning in for the night. The lamplight was a golden glow that bathed the otherwise greyscale surroundings in a slither of hope and warmth and cosiness. The stillness of the hour, despite the giant clock on the wall, was calming. Nia had already begun to doze off in a pile of sheets of paper.

Bella shook her gently. "Nia, I need to tell you something."

Nia yawned and scratched her head. "Sure, what's up?" Her voice was groggy, and distant.

"Nia, this is serious," she said, "it's about the escape."

She straightened up, and when she saw Bella's concerned face, realised this really *was* serious.

"Okay, what's wrong?"

"When we get over that wall, we don't know how many of us will make it to the other side, or what is actually waiting for us when we get there. Outside of the city, and of the camp, the world is a complete mystery to us both." She scratched the side of her nose and perched on the mattress next to Nia. "I know I speak big of this revolution, but the truth is, I don't know what the next step is after this. We might make newspaper headlines and become enemies of the Government, we might be silenced, and have our records destroyed, be completely ignored. There's an element of risk with this."

"Bella, we knew all along there would be risk -"

"Yeah, but just listen, okay?" Her gaze was stern. "Make it to somewhere safe in the woods, hide there until we know what situation we're dealing with, and work on a revolution from there." Nia nodded as she followed Bella's words. "But there's a farm, okay? It's right at the edge of the Territory, right at the edge of the city. A haven, like an end goal, or a halfway point, I guess. *Appleby Farm* it's called, alright? You got that?"

"Yeah, I got it. Appleby farm." Nia looked at her in confusion.

"Go to the edge of the farm, at the entrance you'll see a large farmhouse, beaten old bricks, and a really large chicken shed, okay? But at the entrance, where the gate is already swung open, just leap across it, and it'll lead to another path, alright? There's a cave there, right at the end, beside a tiny slaughtering house with a tin roof. In the cave there's enough food, blankets, knives, whatever, to keep four people alive for six months, and one person alive...indefinitely, depending on how it's rationed."

"Bella, why are you telling m–"

"If you get into any shit, Nia, I want you to go there. Promise me, okay? Promise me you'll go there."

"Bella–"

"*Promise.*"

"Okay." Nia gulped. "If anything happens, I'll go there."

Bella nodded and took a deep breath. "Okay, good. I'll leave you details and stuff on the night we leave, and have a map drawn up and stuff."

"Why would we be safe there?"

"Cause it's my home." Bella smiled. "My dad was prepared for anything and everything. And he knew before I came here what I was going to start. So, he made sure that I could still come home afterwards, and still be safe. No one will be able to find that cave unless they know where it is. And I need you to know about it too in case I don't make it over that wall."

"Bella, don't be silly–"

"I'm not being silly, Nia." She sighed. "I'm being realistic. Looking at the shaky plan we have, and at my physical capabilities, compared to that of Jay, you, Eddie, and especially Veronika. There's countless obstacles we'll face on the way out, numerous soldiers that will shoot us down."

"Bella, hush." Nia put an arm around her. "We are in this together," she said sternly. "You are the one who got me to realise that this cause is important to the lives of everyone, and so I am *not* going to be the one to leave you behind. You can shut the fuck up with that talk right now."

"Nia..."

"I said shut the fuck up, Bella." Nia laughed. "You're coming with us, okay?"

Bella pursed her lips and held her tongue. She tried to find a smile, but it didn't quite reach her eyes.

"Okay."

CHAPTER FORTY-
THREE

9 DAYS BEFORE

E ddie saw the sheets twisted around Nia in such a way that it framed her figure beautifully. It was almost a week before they were due to leave, and Eddie found himself feeling oddly attached to the world he had grown up in. It was not that he agreed with the way it worked, or anything of that sort. It was that it was familiar, and certain, and that in the moments that were passing as he gazed at Nia, asleep and restful, he felt so unbelievably happy. Why could it not stay like this, forever?

He stood at the foot of the bed, entirely naked except for his military tags that he wore around his neck. He knew he needed to be strong. Stronger than ever. He feared that breaking out of the camps would be his hardest test yet.

What would his father think? What would his mother think? His colleagues, his friends - would they suspect it?

Probably not.

He could imagine the way they would cover it up. Either as a hostage situation, or a severe case of mania. His father being in the public eye, they could not simply erase his records. Eddie could picture headlines, front pages with photographs of his grieving and disappointed parents, with quotes such as:

"We just want our son to return to us."

"We can't believe this has happened"

"The mania has changed him. He is not the man we once knew."

Eddie would have let them down. He was going to have to accept that. His father would be angry, would lash out wildly in his study, throwing about books and ornaments, like he had so often done in a rage. He would deny ever having a son, deny ever knowing Eddie, deny ever caring for him. While his mother would simply sit and silently weep.

It broke his heart, just a little. Because although his parents were, by anyone's recommendations, bad people, they were still his parents.

Eddie sighed, and looked back at the bed. Nia's blonde hair was strewn across the scarlet sheets. She clutched a pillow to her chest, tucked underneath her chin.

He walked barefoot across the rug to the bedside table. He pulled out the drawer and right at the back, was a tiny scarlet leather box, with a golden rim. He plucked it out from where it had been tossed, haphazardly, some years ago. He then paced back to the window-ledge as he looked out at the usual view.

Eddie prized open the stiff lid with a quiet crunch of leather. The diamond ring glinted spectacularly in the light from the moon. It was tucked delicately between the cheeks of a black velvet cushion.

His mother had given it to him on his eighteenth birthday, three years prior. A family heirloom that had been his great-great-grandmother's, before she died. She had apparently requested that the jewelled ring should be inherited by each first born in the family. She had been given it by her husband before they married, before arrangements were made on behalf of prospective couples. Eddie's mother had instructed him that he was to give it to the woman that was chosen for him, when their time came to marry. At the time, he was disgusted at the thought - and still was, to an extent. He had hated the idea that the woman he was supposed to spend the rest of his life with, have children with, would be one that he had not chosen himself. His judgement did not appear valued, the whims of his heart overshadowed. He had cast the diamond to the back of his drawer and prayed to not have to live to see it again.

But that evening he had felt a nudge of curiosity in the direction of the diamond. He looked at it, curiously. He had no plans to use it anytime soon, of course. But, if they were leaving in only a week, there would be no harm in taking it with him...

"Eddie?"

He snapped the box shut.

"Hmm?" he said, sliding it onto the window ledge behind a potted plant. In the dark it could not be seen. "Did I wake you?"

"Nah, bad dream," she whispered.

He slid into the bed opposite her, under the sheets, and pulled her a little closer to him. She smelled like salted air and freshly washed sheets.

"What was it about?"

"The usual – death, dying, and the dead." She laughed, without humour. "It's amazing how they can get inside our heads like that. I'm glad we'll be away from it soon."

Eddie chose his words carefully. "Yeah, me too. The woods will offer some protection for a time, I would imagine."

There was a long moment of stillness. There was nothing but heat and the sound of breathing, and the ounce of safety that came with lying next to someone you care for in the dark.

"What are we doing?" Nia asked.

"What do you mean?"

She propped herself up slightly. "Is this a good idea?" she asked. "Us?"

Eddie looked confused. "You're not enjoying my company?"

"That's not what I mean." She traced a line down between his collarbones. "I mean – this whole movement is *so* risky. Do we really want to add onto that the complications of being in a relationship? The... leverage that could be used against us? Aren't we just adding to the list of things that they can use to hurt us?"

She looked scared – perhaps more scared of his reaction than of the scene she was describing. Her eyes were wide, shining white in the darkness as they reflected the little light that there was. Her eyebrows stitched together in worry. Despite this, her hand clutched to his tightly, as if she was afraid he was going to go away.

"The way I see it," Eddie answered, "is that we are making ourselves happy by being together. And if us being together doesn't harm anyone else, then there is no problem with that, whatsoever."

"There isn't?"

"Of course not," he answered. "Be it me and you, or two guys in the third year, or two old ladies in their last years. Be it romantic love, friendship love, family love - it's not a weakness. It's a brilliant, pure, amazing thing. And I think the world needs more of people who are together because they genuinely love each other, and appreciate each other, and want to make each other's lives better. We can't have more bitter loveless marriages like my mum and dad who are together because they have to be. It rots the soul. It's unnatural to spend your life with someone you hate."

Her face relaxed. "You speak wise words, Eddie," she said. "You are one of the creators of the revolution, after all. Maybe you really can write a good speech."

He laughed. "When I have to, yeah."

She clutched his face and kissed him delicately on the lips. For such a long second it felt like the rest of the world had vanished.

"Are you scared?" she said, as she leaned away again.

"A little." He rolled over and stretched out his back. "But I think we have a pretty stable team. We'll do good. All we're missing really is doctor. It's a shame about Doctor Schiffer. She would have been ideal."

Nia sighed and rolled into the perfect crescent under Eddie's arm, where her shoulder and neck and the lines of her body seemed to fit so comfortably. As she drifted off to sleep, her mind stayed fixated on Doctor Schiffer. Then, like the quick and electrifying buzz that the blue light of a flytrap might make, she had an idea.

CHAPTER FORTY-FOUR

7 DAYS BEFORE

C harles sat at his bedroom desk. It was identical to all those in the dorm rooms around him, but with double the amount of work to do.

He had been working for hours, and the pile of study materials appeared to get no smaller at all. There was so much he needed to know. Why couldn't he just be told what was important and necessary for him to be a doctor and leave it at that? Skip the rest of the tests, like additional mathematics, and the history of the Dictator. None of it felt like it mattered, and it was just adding so much additional work to his load that he didn't want to do.

He wondered whether he could confront his professors, and ask for a lower workload in other subjects, considering he already knew what he wanted to do. He could ask his biology professor whether the additional medical training couldn't wait until after his initial training at the camps – but both scenarios sounded too difficult, too risky, and would lead to bad consequences he would have to live with.

He sat back in his chair and pushed back the loose strand of hair that always fell back over his face whenever he leaned forward. He rubbed the back of his neck, and his shoulder muscle, which was sore from writing.

If only there were a way for him to learn in his own time, at his own pace, and learn only the things he wanted to.

There was a knock at the door. He was thankful for the opportunity to stand, and stretch, and answered the call.

Two girls he recognised filled his doorframe.

"Charles, right?"

Nia's face was serious, but her eyes were bright and excitable.

"We need to talk to you."

CHAPTER FORTY-FIVE

5 DAYS BEFORE

Veronika had been raised by her mum and her grand-mother.

Her father had been taken gravely ill when she was very young - an incurable illness - and had been humanely taken care of by the Authorities. Apparently there had been a very big send-off for him, as he was a very hardworking man. They had wanted to make an example of him and have him fondly remembered. Veronika had been so young that she didn't remember any of it. She didn't even know what his face looked like.

Her mother hardly spoke about it. She had shut it away in a box in her mind and thrown away the key. Her mother's attitude was that being weighed down by grief only made her less able to do the things she needed to do. She wasn't going to let the past decide that her future was bleak - it was bleak enough as it was.

Instead, Veronika's mother had thrown herself into her work. She distracted herself with her role in the Agricultural Sector and cared for her own mother in the mornings and evenings around work. Veronika's mother knew that she was nothing but a number to the Government. She knew that it had been the same for her husband. She found the money they threw at the funeral insulting. They had been in the newspaper for weeks both on the lead up and after his death. Then, once the interest surrounding their story had diminished, the Government had never sent her a letter of condolence or checked up on her. They had not set up any form of support. They used her and her husband for their story, to better the reputation of the Dictator. Then left her in the dust, with a one-year-old daughter, an aging mother, and no husband's hand to hold throughout it all.

"We are nothing but things to them," she had whispered, some nights, in the dark. Veronika hadn't known what it meant at the time. She had simply enjoyed being in the same bed as her mum, hiding under the covers from the darkness. She had enjoyed it when they told each other made up stories before bedtime. Fictional nonsense to take their minds to better places. It hid the hurt well.

Veronika's mother didn't like to dwell in the past. She had always been about the present moment.

"The past can only hurt you if you let it."

Veronika tried to remember this often. She tried to not let the past creep in. It was a week before they were supposed to break out of Camp Clandestine, and Veronika was trying hard to keep her mind focused on the present, and on the future. She wanted to keep the goal in mind. She was excited at the promise of different, potentially better things.

But it was like her brain was a spinning top. She could get it going, keep it spinning, keep it balanced. And when it was balanced, it was smooth and beautiful and clean. But when gravity took a hold on it, when the momentum behind it stopped, she would topple. She would slip. She would come crashing down.

On the morning before Veronika had left to get the train, it had only been her grandmother who had been there to wave her goodbye from the front porch. She was sat in her wheelchair, her wrinkled, kind eyes welling with tears. Her liver spotted hands had given her a squeeze.

"Off you go now, dear."

Veronika had been well aware that her grandmother would not likely be there when she returned - *if* she returned. Three years was a long time. Her grandmother was not young. She had a feeling that it was knowledge they both shared but didn't speak of.

Veronika tried not to think about it when she was at the Camps. She tried not to think about her grandmother, or her mother. She needed to focus. She needed to leave those things behind her. When this was all over, they wouldn't be around for her to celebrate with. She knew this. She wanted to make *sure* she knew this. Whatever else the others were doing this for - to see their parents, to choose who they loved, to live without fear - Veronika wasn't doing it for those reasons. She was doing it because she had nothing else to lose. They had already stripped her of everything she had ever loved. She worked hard every day because there was simply no alternative.

Veronika Shaw knew that this was a cause worth fighting for, for the masses. She knew that very few people would risk getting involved, especially this early on, because there was so much at stake.

But for Veronika, that simply was not the case.

She had nothing to lose, everything to gain, and everything to give.

It was time to see how strong she really was.

CHAPTER FORTY-SIX

6 HOURS BEFORE

He found himself continuously checking his hands. Did he get underneath the nails well enough? Were there any traces left in the cracks of his skin?

He picked at under his fingernails, without even thinking about it. He felt fixated on it. On her face. On the noises she'd made.

Had he made the right decision? Had he done the right thing?

He got up and went to the sink again.

Had she really deserved that?

He picked up the soap.

Had he really been capable of it?

He turned on the hot water.

What had he been *thinking*?

He began to scrub. His skin was already pink and sore, but he couldn't stop himself. He felt frayed, uncertain. He was scared of what his hands had done. He was scared of the possibilities that this now held.

Was he a bad person? Was he under their spell? Or was he Curious?

He bit at a tough bit of skin that lurked around one of his fingernails. He bit at it until it came off. He bit at it until it bled.

Dan had never done anything like this before. He had been unphased when disposing of Martin's body, when it had been an order. But when it had made the decision on his own, it was an action that had made him feel sick to his stomach.

Stephanie had been innocent. She hadn't done anything wrong. Why had he stopped her? Why had he felt the need to stop her, and to do so in such a way?

Dan didn't consider himself to be Curious. If what she had said was true, and there was talk of a group of individuals leaving, Dan would not go with them. Would he?

No, of course not. That was suicide. That was stupid. He would simply be voluntarily deciding to end his life. And that would be such a waste - he was a Supreme Cadet. He had great potential. They had told him this on several occasions. He had a fantastic career in the military lined up for him. He had higher chances of gaining a beautiful, perfect partner match for himself. His future looked positive.

Didn't it?

Dan grabbed the towel and dried his hands. They stung from the soap and the scrubbing. He told himself he needed to stop now. The blood was gone. Stephanie was gone. He needed to move past this.

What had he feared? Had he thought that with Stephanie reporting Nia and the others that he would somehow get wrapped up in it?

Maybe.

He had witnessed Nia using the Prohibited Web and hadn't stopped her. He'd *helped* her, even. Yes. That must be it. He did it to protect himself.

But Stephanie didn't know about what he had done. And Dan trusted that Nia would feel no need to drag him into it if they had been arrested and interrogated. Dan had done nothing wrong. He'd just stood and looked at an empty corridor. He hadn't really asked many questions. He'd paid an interest, but he still didn't know for certain what Nia was up to. Nobody knew for certain. Stephanie certainly couldn't have known - not from the few minutes of conversation that she overheard. She must have misinterpreted it. She must have done.

Then why had he killed her?

Dan didn't know who he had been protecting. He hadn't really thought about it. He had felt an instinctive protectiveness - not just towards Nia, but to the whole group. Why did Stephanie feel the need to get involved? It was her fault, really, for listening in when she shouldn't have been.

Yeah, it was Stephanie's own fault that she was dead.

Dan tried to nod to himself to reaffirm the thought, but no matter how hard he tried, it just wouldn't stick.

He couldn't come to terms with it. What he was done, or why he had done it. He could not accept the reality of it all.

Deep down, he knew. He just refused to believe it.

He was fighting it. Everything he had ever been told, and everything his true self actually believed, was conflicted. He didn't know what to believe. The world around him, so blaringly obvious and blaringly miserable, or the voice in his head - so quietly stubborn, and obnoxiously hypnotic.

The light disappeared and was replaced by darkness outside his window. He paced his room all night, not getting a wink of sleep. He wandered the grounds, with no purpose and no direction, only confused and misguided thoughts.

He found a room, abandoned, and adorned with expensive furnishings. He needed different scenery, a place to properly think. He took his gun with him. He wasn't sure why. He thought maybe, if the thinking drove him mad enough, he could just end it all there, by his own choosing, and repent for his sins.

He stayed there in the darkness for a very long time.

CHAPTER FORTY-SEVEN

30 MINUTES BEFORE

Nia stood in her room, alone.

The lights were off. The room was dark, and the silver spotlight of the moon reflected boldly from the large clock face. The huge hands were pointed at the numbers eleven and six.

Just thirty minutes to go.

It had all boiled down to this. Every moment of every day since she had stepped foot inside the grounds of Camp Clandestine. Almost five months. This is what every early morning and every long night had led to.

Her mind felt surprisingly calm. Her stomach, on the other hand, was doing somersaults of its own accord. Whenever she swallowed, it was as if she was trying to stop herself from being sick.

Nerves can do that to you.

The last meal she had eaten that evening had been some kind of casserole. She hadn't dared ask what was. It had been a very different meal compared to the first morning she had spent at the camp, way back in Autumn. That evening she had been relatively confident and comfortable, and had finished her meal, knowing it might be the last one she had for a while. She thought she had seen Bella sneaking some of her potatoes into a napkin, and subtly stuffing it into a bag by her feet.

The leaves on the trees were starting to regrow, and to blossom into flowers. The night was warmer too. The past few nights had been stuffy, especially when packed into a building so huge. The heat of all those bodies builds up into extra discomfort.

That evening however, there were but a few dark clouds littering the sky. It was a rare form of night, but the harsh winds of the day had shifted the pollution, and stars could be seen twinkling up there in the darkness. It made the night chillier, and Nia got excited by this idea. It was the kind of chill that wasn't enough to make you feel cold but was just enough to make your hairs stand on end and your body shiver every now and again involuntarily. It was the kind of chill that made you want to *move.*

In the huge glass of the clock, Nia could see her own reflection. She was dressed entirely in black, in the outdoor weather gear they had provided for her. The trousers were advertised as being warm, breathable, and weather-proof, as was the coat to match. The boots she wore were strong, flexible and comfortable. But, most importantly – practical. Sturdy, with a rough-textured sole for extra grip, and ankle supports for climbing and running. She had tied the laces that night with a double knot, to make sure they did not come undone.

Her hair she had pulled back into a long braid, that started right at the front of her head, and encased every hair all the way down to just below her shoulder blades.

She had hidden behind that hair every day of her life. She stood there and thought about everything she was going to be doing in the next however-many years, and what it would represent, and how she wanted to be seen. She thought about the opportunities she would be given, and what that meant for her, and whether simply having the hair to hide behind was an option she wanted.

She held in her hands a pair of scissors. The blades were

sharp and glinted in the moonlight.

She didn't hesitate. She placed her long braid in the centre of the shears and clamped down hard. Her hair fell to the ground. She continued to snip, to chop, to demolish everything she had grown for the past nineteen years of her life and looked into the glass at the reflection of the new person she now saw before her.

The hair she had left was short round the back and sides, was practical, and hung longer on one side just above her eye. It was messy and not in the least unified or approved of. But she had done it herself. Because she wanted to. Because no one was there to tell her not to.

Nia looked at herself and saw the face of the revolution. She saw rebellion and standing up for what was right.

She left her hair where it had landed on the dark grey floorboards. The long hand on the clock crept closer and closer towards the twelve.

Someone could die tonight, she thought, as she grabbed her rucksack and watched the clock reach the first strike of midnight.

And someone would.

EMBLEMATIC (ADJ.)

Used to describe something which is symbolic; a meaningful representation of something else.

Each of the Rebellious took one personal item with them that night. Some for reasons unknown, others for reasons with a little more clarity. They had each agreed on what supplies they would all be in charge of, what should be taken, and what should be left behind. But one thing was for certain: they were only allowed one item that was not practical, one thing that held value in their hearts, rather than in their heads.

Nia took her diary with her, which I am probably most thankful for out of everyone. Nia had decided in the time she had spent at the camps, and in the run up to the escape, that she did not want any reminder of the life she used to lead, and that it was probably safer for her family if nothing could be traced back to them. She did not want the association. She wanted to make it as easy as possible for the Government to erase her completely – it was what she wanted. Without that diary, I would not be sitting where I am today, sharing the knowledge that I now have. Nia knew that the documentation of events was of importance. She was a very practical young lady.

Eddie took the engagement ring that was once his grandmother's. It was the only item he owned that he felt needed to be saved and cherished. Every other luxury item he owned he held no attachment to. His grandmother, however, was a memory he wanted to hold onto. The ring served as a reminder of the future he wanted.

Veronika took a bright purple scarf that had once been her mother's. It had originated from the style of clothing that her ancestry descended from. Bright colours, magnificent patterns and beautiful craftsmanship. It would bring her warmth and comfort, and she figured it could be used as bandages too, if the need came for it. For now, she tied it round her head, like a bandana, to keep the hair out of her eyes.

Jay took his harmonica. It was his father's. He had been given very little opportunity to play it since arriving at the camps. He liked the idea of having a form of entertainment for the long days when they would be in hiding.

Charles took a tattered photograph of his family - he wasn't quite ready to be without them. He thought it was important that he remembered where he began, where he came from, and who he was going to be fighting for. He was the most uncertain of all the rebellious. He still needed his reminder of why he had agreed to take part.

And Bella, the maker of it all, took a long white feather from her father's chicken farm which she often used as a bookmark.

The feather would later become the symbol of the revolution.

PIVOTAL (ADJ.)

Of crucial importance in relation to the development of something else, such as a plan, or story.

Nia followed her copy of the map to be sure she avoided each of the cameras on the way down the stairs. The night was crisp and still when she made it outside. She used the window of the canteen rather than the door, and sneaked along the edge below the glass, so as not to be seen if anyone were looking out. Then, a quick climb up the wall to reach the wire to the camera on the corner. A sharp tug, to cut it off from the rest of the circuit, and she cut across the pathway without being seen.

It was around the back of the Assembly Hall building, hidden behind the large waste bins there, that they had agreed to meet. One of the few spots in the entire vicinity that contained absolutely no recording devices, lights, anything.

It was quiet, still, and dark. This darkness however was anything but comforting. There was a buzzing in the air. The unsettling, nervous energy that lingers like mist before an important event.

It was here that all six of the rebellious met for the first time. They exchanged pleasantries and discussed the plan of how they were going to escape.

It was confirmed to everyone's lack of ease, that it would be very difficult to get out of the camps without being seen by anyone. But they were still going to try.

Eddie handed out the few guns he had managed to smuggle and told everyone to use their bullets sparingly where possible. In the event that it was kill-or-be-killed everyone was instructed to pull the trigger.

They made a pact. Swore an oath to one another that this was for the good of the people, swore that if tonight someone was to fall behind, they are to be left behind.

They scuttled off into the darkness, leaving behind them on the floor, written in red paint:

"FREEDOM FOR ALL – The Rebellious"

Beside it was a red splatter resembling the shape of a feather.

CHAPTER FORTY-EIGHT

THAT NIGHT

Nia ducked underneath a small wall as the roaming light beam streamed across the courtyard of the dorms. It was dazzlingly bright, so she was sure not to look at it in case it ruined her vision. Behind her was Charles and Jay. On the opposite side of the courtyard, hidden in the darkness somewhere, were Eddie, Bella and Veronika.

They sprinted along in the shadows, getting closer to the perimeter, when Charles tugged on Nia's jacket.

She looked at him, questioning, and saw a pale and terrified face staring back at her.

"I think I'm going to be sick," Charles whispered.

"Okay but do it quietly."

With the faint smell of vomit in the air, Nia took in what she could see.

A few metres in front of Eddie, there was a single guard stood just outside of the shadows cast by the building. In the occasional sweeping of the blinding light, the black uniformed man could be seen. His helmet off, holding a sinister-looking gun, and a cigarette in one gloved hand. Beyond him there was the sports halls, with the shipping containers that held the training equipment standing sturdily in the dark, just behind the floodlit assault course.

The plan was to sneak behind the shipment containers, and make their way behind the buildings beyond them. Then they would sneak beneath the watchtower, and around to the only part of the wall covering the perimeter that had a tree stood next to it. The tree would be used as a step-up to leap over the ten-foot wall, and into the woods beyond.

Nia watched Eddie from where they crouched, as he crept along the edge of the wall towards the unsuspecting guard. In one swift movement that Nia nearly missed it was so quick, Eddie wrapped both arms around the man's head and pulled him down. Her eyes were torn away as Jay did the same thing to the man a few metres away from them.

The man kicked and scuffled slightly in Jay's firm grip. His elbow was tucked and tightening underneath the man's chin, his other hand wrapped around his skull, holding his head still. When the man tried to kick, Jay leapt and wrapped his legs around his opponent's. He wrestled him to the ground, detaining him. In the still night, it sounded like such a racket, and Nia was worried that I would draw attention to them all. But soon enough, the man fell still, and collapsed in a heavy heap. The cigarette glowed orange where it lay discarded in the gravel.

"Oh my gosh," Nia whispered.

"Kill or be killed," Jay muttered.

They journeyed on.

The two groups joined as they turned the corner by the assault course, and headed left, keeping close to the buildings. There was another guard stood at the corner furthest away from them, and Veronika motioned for everyone to stay low and quiet. They crept along beside the edge of the sports hall with little difficulty, keeping themselves low beneath the windows of the buildings.

They did not know however, that a Supreme Cadet was stood on the opposite side of the glass, watching their every move with curious eyes. He knew what he should do in a situation like this, but found himself hesitating for a very long moment. He knew who they were. But he was still unsure exactly what they were doing.

Nia continued further on, following the lead of Eddie and Bella.

"This way," Bella turned to whisper to the group. "We head behind the shipping containers with the training equipment, and duck along the fence there – not many cameras. Once we get around to the Watch Tower, Eddie will be able to pull the plug on the electronics in the area, shutting off all the cameras and lights, so we should be able to get across the field and over the wall with no trouble."

It sounds like such a perfect plan.

"Ready?"

Flawless...

"Follow me."

...Almost.

"Shit!" Veronika whispered, grabbing Bella by the collar and shoving her into the wall. She pointed, and the others saw it too – the alley they had been about to sprint down had two guards, each with their own burley and sinister-looking dog. The dogs already looked like they had sniffed something was not right, and the guards were turning on their torches and scouring the edges of the alley.

"They'll see us," Charles squeaked.

"Quick!" Eddie used his key-card to open the door to the closest building. "Everyone – through here!"

The six of them snuck through into the building, quietly shutting the door behind them and catching their breath.

The room they found themselves in looked something like a living room. There was a stone fireplace, surrounded by book-cases. Comfy armchairs arranged neatly on an antique-looking rug, with side tables and polished lamps. It was very much like an 1800s gentleman's club. Nobody knows to this day what went on in that room on a day-to-day basis.

"Fuck me, this is hard." Jay rubbed his forehead, speaking softly. "How much longer have we got of this?"

"Never mind that, where do we head from here?" Veronika asked. "Our way out is blocked."

They all looked between themselves, then at Bella and Eddie.

"Do we turn back?" Charles asked.

"Mate, we just killed two people between us." Jay shook his head. "We can't turn back. Imagine the kind of search they'll have tomorrow – I'm getting the fuck outta here."

Eddie nodded in agreement. "He's right. We have to keep going forward. If we head out of the other side of the building, we'll be at the training fields. Can't turn right towards our previously designated route, because the Watch Tower will see us before we get to it. But if we turn left, then there's a chance we can cut close to the back of the student housing building."

"What's at the back of the student housing building?" Nia asked.

"It's a small walkway, enclosed between a four-foot wall, and the edge of the building itself. If I'm correct then there should have been a delivery today, and they use the back alley to store various crates and boxes. We could probably duck down there and use the boxes as cover."

"Cover for what, exactly?" Veronika's face was stern.

"From soldiers," Bella answered. "It's a dark alleyway – there will be a load of security down there. My map says there's at least two cameras as well that we can't hide from."

"We'll be spotted?" Charles gulped. Nia saw he was visibly quivering, and still as equally pale and pasty as he had been prior to vomiting.

"Look, we knew this was a possibility from the start," Bella explained calmly. "We're just going to have to risk it. We're all armed, right?"

BANG. A gunshot.

"Shit!"

Everybody ducked down to the floor. There, stood in the doorway to the next room was the same Supreme Cadet that had spotted them a few moments before. In his steady hands he held a gun, which he was pointing, in turn, at each of the six escapees.

"What are you doing?" he asked. He was clearly confused and uncertain of what he was doing. His hair was short and especially dark, his face still holding a roundness and innocence that is associated with childhood, despite the dark sketching of facial hair that littered his cheeks and mouth. He was of stocky build, with muscular shoulders, and his skin appeared incredibly pale in the dim light. It was hard to tell from where he stood in the shadows, but Nia was sure she had seen him before around the campus.

"Dan?"

"Step back," he said.

"Is anyone hurt?" Eddie asked. His question was met with subtle shakes of heads. Everyone was fine. Nobody dared look away from the gun that was pointed at them.

"What are you doing in here, mate?" Eddie said.

The guy twitched slightly at being addressed. "What's it to you?" he spat. "I heard you saying you'd killed people tonight. What's that about?"

"His name's Daniel," Nia said. "He sat next to me in Information Technology."

Dan looked across at her, and she saw a note of calm flicker across his gaze. She saw his gun lower an inch.

"Yeah, I did." He appeared to relax slightly, but his expression was no less manic than it had been before. He looked like he was on the verge of a mental breakdown. "What are you guys doing?"

Nobody answered. They all looked at each other with uncertainty.

Dan's eyes flicked from Eddie's face, to the faces of the other five witnesses in the room. He had never felt more uncertain in his life. They did not appear threatening, nor evil, nor like they would hurt him. Yet their silence was unsettling.

"What are you *doing*?" he demanded.

"Eddie, we're going to have to move, the sound of the gun-shot –"

"Shut up!" Daniel yelled, his face twitching. "Answer me!"

"We're getting out of here."

The gun moved back up to the inch that it was before. "But no one can leave," Dan said, confused.

"We are. We're breaking out."

Nia looked at the others, hesitantly. Torch lights shone at the window outside. "Eddie…"

"Dan, just let us go, okay? Please. We won't hurt you. Just let us go. Pretend you didn't see us."

"Ed, we don't have time for this!" Veronika yelled. She raised her pistol quickly and fired. Dan screamed and dropped his gun, as blood began to pour from the centre of his palm.

It was chaos. Veronika sprinted from the room, followed by a terrified Charles, a determined Bella, and a hesitant Eddie. Dan kneeled on the antique carpet, clutching his right hand, with blood seeping through his fingers and dripping to the floor.

"We need to help him!" Nia exclaimed.

"No, Nia," Jay answered, as men started hammering at the door from outside, "we need to *go*."

Jay heaved one of the chairs across the entranceway as a barricade. The guards from outside shoved furiously. They would burst through it any second.

"Come with us," Nia said to Dan. She crouched down beside him. "You could join us. Fight against these people for your right to choose. We shouldn't have to live in fear!"

Dan's green eyes gazed up at her. His wounded hand shook from the pain. Blood oozed out from underneath his clenched fist and dripped onto the antique carpet. He tried to speak, but found his tongue was paralysed with shock. He looked at the wound, at the blood. His stomach felt heavy, his lips numb.

"Nia, c'mon!" Jay yelled, before grabbing Nia by the hand

and giving it a yank.

Dan watched them leave through the next room, then the adjoining door into the street outside. Nia looked back twice to where he knelt in the dark.

Dan watched through the window as the group continued their way. The blindingly fluorescent light of the Watch Tower continued to sweep by like an ominous lighthouse, causing him to wince. It was blindly bright, casting every shadow into dazzling exposure. The shock eased.

He had an idea.

The guards continued to thump furiously at the door. But when they eventually broke through, the room was entirely empty.

Bella snuck out first, following Eddie's instructions. They crept low underneath the windows, below the wall in the darkness, her pistol was ready. She thought of how they had left Dan bleeding, and wondered if he would follow, and if he even could. She could still hear the thumping of the guards as they tried to get through Jay's makeshift barricade.

That was when the siren started.

It was a shrill, loud ringing bell. A sound that every cadet was trained from day one to recognise as the noise signifying an attack.

"For fuck's *sake!*" Bella muttered, under her breath. "Guys! Let's *fucking* move!"

She reached the corner, the start of the alley, and paused to look at what they were dealing with. The noises continued to build up – the bell, the thumping, and now the overhead announcement speakers:

"Caution: the campus is under attack."

"*Fuck* this *fucking* army camp!" Veronika cursed from behind, as the thumping stopped, the door burst open, and Jay, Veronika and Eddie shot dead the four men that came charging through.

"That felt good." Veronika grinned.

Bella snuck down. The alley was exactly as Eddie had described. Littered with crates, boxes, and – as far as she could tell – only four guards. But all of them were heading this way.

Bella did not hesitate. She crouched behind a crate and balanced her gun on top of it. She took a slow, steady breath, and was reminded of the day her father had first taught her how to shoot.

Everything seemed to slow down, to quieten, as her mind focused. Her heartbeat was slow. Her hands were steady.

Bella's emerald eyes were bright as she fired at the first guard. She was struck in the ribcage and staggered backwards slightly, before Bella pulled the trigger again and hit her in the stomach. She collapsed almost instantly.

Bella heard movement ahead. Talking, panic at the sound of the gunshot. The sound of heavy boots getting nearer from in front of her. She heard movement from behind as she scuttled forward. The rest of the team rearranging themselves as her backup.

She hid, stood close to the shadows, and listened intently. There was two of them. Two men, this time. They didn't know where she was, but they knew she was near.

She steadied her breath, pictured them in her mind, and, as quick as anything, ducked up from her cover space. She shot them both in the head.

They fell to the ground with surprisingly little noise.

"Holy *shit*, Bella," she heard Veronika say. "You're *good!*"

There were more footsteps from behind, as well as one last person to take down from in front. The moments passed in a blur of gunshots, as the gang of six took down at least one guard each. Charles had to pause again to throw up.

"I shot someone," he said, trembling.

"And we're all very proud of you," Jay said, his patience wearing thin. "Now let's get moving, while we can!"

They ran along the passageway in the dark, listening to the

chaos unfurl around them. With every step they took, their hearts beat faster and more proudly. The fluidity of the emotions - fear and excitement - splashed back and forth within their stomachs. Each of them went from wanting to jump for joy, to wanting to curl over like Charles had done and chuck-up their last meal.

As Bella ran, however, she was a little different to the rest. Her face resembled that of a child who was playing pretend. Free from cares, free from worry, and enthralled by the situation that she was engulfed by at that moment. Her mind's eye was blanketing everything in an aura of wonder and adventure. Her final goal, one which she had been working towards for so long now, was within arm's reach. The beginning of her next chapter, her next life. Changing the lives of so many people, changing the country for the better, freeing the lives and choices and thoughts of everyone she knew, and everyone *they* knew. They were all so close to the starting line.

"It's just around this corner. Then–" She stopped, abruptly. "Shit."

The others stumbled to a halt behind her. Blocking their path was a huge cargo container. It completely covered the rest of the alley, stretching some fifteen feet in the air. Impossible to climb. They had reached a dead-end.

"*No,*" Bella gasped, "No, no, *no*. It wasn't supposed to go like this!"

"What do we do?"

"Calm down, it's okay!"

"But *what do we do*?" Bella breathed, desperately. "They're going to catch us!"

"Up here!" Jay placed his back to the wall and interlocked his fingers. Veronika took the hint instantly, using Jay's hands as a lift, she threw herself up and over the wall.

"Quickly!" They heard her yell from the other side, followed by the sound of several gunshots.

They all followed. Bella leaped over, then watched as Eddie pulled Jay up and over as well.

She turned, to see that they had landed at the far edge of the open training field. The Watch Tower beam continued to sweep over the area – until it found them.

"Shit, shit, *shit!*" Eddie hissed. "Make a run for it!"

The blinding light stayed on them as they sprinted along the wall, as fast as their feet could carry them. Shouts and voices and gunshots could be heard from the distance, each of them skimming the wall just after they passed them. Red brick dust pattered to the ground and into their hair.

It seemed unrealistic, impossible even, that they would make it out of there before one of them was shot.

But then the light went out, and the entire field was plunged into darkness.

A few of them paused, their eyes adjusting, before being shoved along by Eddie.

"It's a miracle!" Bella squeaked, happily.

They looked at the Watch Tower and heard more gun shots. A body was thrown from the top.

They looked ahead.

They could see the tree ahead of them, and its low-hanging branches near the wall. The grass disappeared from beneath their feet as they sprinted towards it, and was replaced by firm, dry and dusty earth. On their right was a chain-link fence, with the dogs from the kennels barking madly at them, snarling with huge teeth, but unable to touch them.

Bella continued to run, as fast as her legs could carry her. She could see the tree, the wall, getting closer and closer with every step.

"Bella!"

She turned, and saw Veronika struggling with a guard. The girl was grappling with her and holding a knife in one hand.

Without hesitation, Bella skidded to a halt and kicked the guard sharply in the back of the leg. The leg buckled, and Veronika grabbed the knife, before jabbing it aggressively into the guard's neck.

"RUN!" Bella screamed.

None of them had ever felt such adrenaline rush through their veins. Bella saw Eddie reach the tree and begin to help Charles up to the branches. Jay was next to follow, hauling himself up and over and onto the other side. Veronika sprinted ahead, and she was the next to leap upwards on the bark.

"Bella!"

It was Nia, she was ahead of her. She had been about to climb over but had stopped. Her eyes were wide in fear, and she was pointing. Bella could feel exactly why.

Flashlights were shining on the back of her head. She could see her own dark shadow stretch across the dusty ground in front of her. She heard the dogs barking furiously, snapped their vicious teeth to her right.

She was so close. Her feet pounded onto the ground. Her heart pounded equally as hard in her chest. She was so close, she could see the tree, she was nearly there.

She reached out a hand to Nia to grab hold. They were inches away from one another, their fingers about to touch.

And then – a gunshot.

It ripped through the centre of her chest like nothing she had ever felt before. The force of her sternum shattering sent her falling to the ground. The dirt grazed her chin, filled her lungs and made her want to cough. The bright lights flashed behind her still and continued to get closer.

Bella saw Eddie grab Nia and shove her upwards, but she protested and tried to fall back, back towards the dearest friend she'd ever had. Nia fell to the ground again, and Eddie's foot slipped. His face was scratched horrifically by branches, brambles and barbed wire, blood pouring from his face. He kept hold of Nia's arm and tried again to shove her upwards. Nia's face was splattered with blood from the gunshot - blood that was not her own.

Bella's ears were filled with a high-pitched ringing noise, as the lights made her vision blurry and blinded. She could see Nia screaming, her face streaming with tears and she yelled at Eddie to let her go. Eddie did not listen to her and pulled her and himself up into the branches of the tree, as more gunshots fired.

Bella watched the two of them safely disappear into the darkness of the woods beyond. The footsteps drew closer by her sides. The lights shone down on her, they ripped her broken backpack from her arms, and moved the hair out of her face. Her chin was soaked in the pool of blood from her bullet wound in the centre of her chest. Her lips were tinged too, as it tried to escape from her mouth.

"State your name and motive," one of them yelled at her.

"Fuck you," she gasped, followed by a weak and trembling laugh. Her smile was drenched in her own blood, but was still the most genuine, happy smile that you would have ever seen.

The guard placed a gun to her head.

"Long live the revolution!" Bella cried.

He pulled the trigger.

INEQUITABLE (ADJ.)

Unfair, unjust.

Bella Lockett is the kind of person that everybody should aspire to be.

She was someone who knew right from wrong, and was not afraid to fight for everything she believed in.

She was someone who loved her parents and wanted nothing more than for them to be safe, happy, and proud of her.

She worked for nearly nineteen years to light a fire in the hearts of her peers, and to open the eyes of those who had been blinded by the propaganda that was forced upon the world.

She died approximately twelve feet away from safety.

She died approximately twelve feet away from her dream.

AFTER

EMPTY (ADJ.)

Having no purpose or value.

The moments that followed were the quietest moments to have ever echoed across the land.

The five of them stood in a mishapen circle, all words escaping their minds. What was there to say? No amount of living, no amount of training, could ever have prepared them for this.

They could only stand and stare through everything, their eyes seeing only the light vanish from Bella's over and over. All they could hear was the sound of that gunshot that had cast her to the floor.

None had looked back. They had taken each other by the hand, the arm, the elbow, and dragged and ran as fast and as far as their legs would take them. They had moved until they could move no more, until the forest was a place so comfortingly unfamiliar that they felt safe.

Here they had come to an unprescedented stop. All together, and all at once. They had stopped, unsure exactly of what to say or what to do.

Nobody had planned what was to happen next. Nobody, that was, except Bella.

The night was a dark inky blue, not a rustle in the trees, not a single life awake in the bushes and long grass surrounding them.

Stillness had never sounded so loud.

LONG LIVE THE REVOLUTION.

ACKNOWLEDGEMENTS

First thing's first: a huge thanks is needed to Leanne, Melissa and Laura for being my wonderful proof-readers, editors and general go-to wonderful people. You have all given me so many ideas, constructive feedback, and encouragement with this novel. You've gone above and beyond for me and Clandestine, and given me such faith in myself and my writing. From the bottom of my heart, I mean it when I say: *this book could never in a million years have happened without you guys. You're the best!*

Thank you to Shannon Lockett. You were the first person I shared this crazy idea with back in the summer of 2016. Without you telling me to go for it, this book would not exist. So a big thank you to you! (And an even bigger thank you for letting me use your name and face in this story!).

Thank you to my husband for all your encouragement and support throughout this writing process. You really are my number one cheerleader. I feel so lucky to have you.

And finally, thank you to everybody who purchased a copy of this book - your support is priceless!

ABOUT THE AUTHOR

V. J. Spencer

In the twenty-odd years V.J. Spencer has been writing she has finished three novels and gained a Masters Degree in Publishing. Vic is an active member in the annual NaNoWriMo challenge, which takes place around the world each November. In 2019 she winged it without having prepped beforehand, and finished her first draft of 'Liberty' four days before the deadline.

Vic hopes to one day be published traditionally. In her spare time she enjoys vegetarian cooking and is currently failing to teach herself how to crochet. Clandestine is her second self-published novel, and the first in the Clandestine Trilogy.

For updates on V.J. Spencer's upcoming novels, or to read her blog, check out her website, and follow her on Instagram:
www.vjspencer.co.uk
@vj_spencer

CALAMITOUS

Coming Soon

Read on for an exclusive preview of the second book in the 'Clandestine' series.

'Calamitous' is due to be released in 2021.

CALAMITOUS (ADJ.)

Catastrophic or disastrous; causing great damage or suffering.

INTERVAL (N.)

A pause or break in activity.

And then there were five.

After commencing my research, I have managed to gather an awful lot of information about The Rebellious. Originally, I thought it would all fit nice and neatly into one book, but apparently, I underestimated just how much work would be needed to document everything that happened. You hold in your hands the second volume. I can only hope that you have recovered from the monumental stress of what happened last.

We join our small troop of Curious Beings after they have successfully completed their escape from Camp Clandestine. They ran for some time, until the shouts and gunshots and sirens disappeared behind them in the shadows. They walked past the rotting bodies of failed cadets, who had been murdered by their lieutenants and fellow students. They had no time to stop, lest they become one of them.

Nia, Eddie, Jay, Veronika and Charles. The fate of the revolution now fell onto them, what with Bella not making it over the wall. Newspapers didn't document her as part of those who escaped – because she didn't. At first, they tried their hardest to hide the fact that there had been a breach. But as time wore on, and the cadets who had witnessed the incident began to talk, it all got out of control.

The Government decided that reporting five Curious beings was far better than reporting six, and so Bella was not mentioned in any reports. All that was mentioned was that one Curious individual was shot dead before they were given the chance to leave the walls of Camp Clandestine. This was a small win for the Government. They did not give the individual a name.

Her name was Bella Lockett. She was the one to start all this. And sadly, she would not be there to finish it.

CHAPTER ONE

Daniel squeezed his injured fist tightly. He had wrapped a strip of cloth around his palm to try and stop the bleeding. The gunshot wound that Veronika had given him had thankfully missed his bones. However, his fingers were still stiff when he tried to move them.

The group had left him there. Nia had asked him to follow. He had wanted to, but at that moment his mind was still torn, much like the tendons in his hand. Being Curious was illegal. Escaping from Camp Clandestine was illegal. A part of his brain simply couldn't let go of the conditioning it had received when he was a child. Breaking the law is punishable by death.

But as soon as the six of them had left the room, he had a moment of clarity. Dan looked at his injured hand – it wasn't that bad. He looked at the life that surrounded him, and the future that awaited him... and that really did look bad.

The lieutenants repeatedly bashed at the door of the building. The group of six disappeared into the shadows out the back. Dan sat on the floor, in between the two groups.

Did he help the lieutenants, and fulfil his duty as a Supreme Cadet? Or did he follow Nia and her friends into the unknown, and potentially find freedom?

He sucked in a breath and climbed to his feet.

He headed for the back door.

They moved fast. Daniel had waited no more than a few minutes before following the group, but as soon as he ventured outside, they were nowhere to be seen. Dan heard the soldiers finally burst through the barricade and into the room where he had just been sitting. He didn't hesitate to hide amongst the shadows. When the exited through the back door, they ran past him, unaware.

And then the siren started.

"Caution: the campus is under attack."

It was loud, ear-splitting. Dan winced and covered his ears. He sprinted as fast as he could along the edge of the building.

The sound of gunshots pattered in the distance. He was grateful that he had taken his gun with him that night. He lifted it from its holster on his hip and held it ready.

Dan didn't know where the rest of the group had headed, but he guessed from the noise that they were making their way down the back of the student housing building. From where he crouched on the corner of the canteen, he could see the training field. He imagined they planned on finding an escape along the wall somewhere. It was a high wall, but with a run up and perhaps a helping hand, he saw it as a viable way to cross the border into the outside world.

The only problem that Dan foresaw was the watchtower.

There were several watchtowers throughout the campus, but the one that Dan could see was the closest to the field. They said it was placed there to protect the campus from attack – such as if the country went to war and the opposition tried to attack the newest recruits. Dan thought otherwise. That night, he knew it would be used to hinder the escape.

The large beam of light was dazzling. It stood several stories off the ground. Like a giant spotlight, it swept over the grass and highlighted the soldiers that were on guard. There weren't many of them, but there were enough.

Daniel began to move. Being on his own rather than a group of six, he found it easier to hide. In the distance, he continued to hear the bang of gunshots, the shouts of soldiers as they were giving out orders. Dan was pleased to see them distracted by their own fear. Whilst they focused on restoring order, he snuck behind them. He reached the training field without having to pull the trigger on his gun once.

"You there – soldier!"

Dan stopped and turned. A lieutenant was approaching him. He had his helmet off.

"Where are you going?" he demanded. "Get with the rest of the troops, you hear? Where's your lieutenant?"

Dan raised his gun and shot him in the head.

At the sound, others from the surrounding area began to approach. Dan sprinted out onto the grass before anybody could see his face.

The beam of light was surveying the perimeter of the field. Back and forth, back and forth it went. A slow, sinister stream. Dan was thankful it wasn't focused close to the tower. He managed to find the ladder without any trouble. The metal was cold and rough. He began to climb.

As Dan ascended the ladder, his mind was racing. He had never imagined he would be doing something like this. What was his plan? He didn't have one. What was he trying to achieve? He wasn't sure. All he knew was that his gun was fully loaded. He had only used one bullet. And when he had fired that one bullet, his hands hadn't shaken, and he hadn't missed.

Halfway up the ladder, Dan could see the group. They were, as he had guessed, along the back of the student housing building. The alley was littered with boxes and crates, which they were hiding behind very well. Dan was amazed that the watchtower beam hadn't figured out that they were there yet. That being said, Dan knew who he was looking for – whereas the operator of the beam didn't.

Dan reached the top just as Veronika, the girl who had shot him, came leaping over the wall.

He had no time to lose.

The beam found them, quick as a heartbeat. Dan heaved his body weight up the remaining rungs of the ladder and landed solidly on the deck of the watchtower. He flung open the metal door, his gun at the ready.

"What the –?"

"Put your weapons down!" he hollered.

There were three of them. They didn't listen to him. The closest to the door lunged for him, unarmed. Dan grappled his shoulders. He swept a sharp kick under the man's legs, toppling him to the ground. With all his body weight, Dan collapsed his knee onto the soldier's windpipe.

The first solider struggled beneath his legs as the second came towards him. She brandished a knife, raised high above her head. She was aiming for Dan's chest. At the last moment, Dan rolled from her line of attack. She plunged the knife deep into the torso of the floored soldier. As she tried to yank it out again, Dan shot her in the stomach.

The third soldier had been struggling to open an ammunition closet. He finally yanked the metal casing open and fumbled with the bullets inside. Dan took the opportunity to look at the controls for the light beam. The dashboard had an intricate number of buttons and switches that he didn't understand. He pressed a few. Nothing happened.

The third soldier was then ready. He brandished his gun in hands that shook. Dan felt no pity for him. As the soldier pulled the trigger, Daniel ducked out of the way. He closed the space between them both in three paces. Wrapping his arm around the arm of his opponent seamlessly, he twisted. The solider was forced to drop gun to the ground. But he fought back. He lunged an elbow at Dan's face, whacking him squarely in the eye. Dan retreated in pain – but made sure to kick the gun as he did so, sending it flying out of the door and down the ladder. It landed on the grass, some eight stories below.

Dan looked out of the window. He saw the whole group had made it over the dividing wall and were now sprinting across the field. He felt a rush of urgency surge through him. The light was still on them – everybody had a clear aim.

Taking advantage of his distracted state, the soldier came for him, beating Dan's face with clenched fists. Dan doubled over but used the opportunity to thump the soldier in the gut several times until he weakened his grip. With a mighty roar, Dan grabbed the soldier's head and began to smack it against the dashboard of the watchtower. Much to his amazement, whichever combination of buttons or switches were pressed, the light went out.

Gunfire down below ceased momentarily. Dan felt a wave of relief, knowing that he had managed to give them at least a fair chance to make their escape. The field had no other lighting – it would be near impossible to shoot them. Every second counted. Soon, the lieutenants would turn on their torches and get the scent hounds. Dan prayed that Nia and her friends were fast runners.

The female soldier stirred. She coughed. She was reaching for something. Dan noticed that the first soldier he had killed still had his gun on his belt.

Dan snatched his gun from its holster and shot her three times. BANG-BANG-BANG. He then turned. The third soldier still had his face pressed against the dashboard. He was bleeding all over the buttons. He raised his gun to shoot.

"Please! Don't! Don't shoot me."

Dan lowered his gun, struck by the plea. He had never heard a lieutenant beg before.

"Okay."

Dan grabbed him and dragged him towards the door. He threw him from the doorway. His body did not look the same when it struck the ground below. Dan waited to see if he felt some form of remorse. He was surprised when it did not come.

The difference between his murdering of Stephanie and the murdering of these lieutenants? It was hard for him to tell. Maybe it was because she had trusted him, and he had outright betrayed her. Both had been a threat to the group escaping. Both had believed in Curiousness being a crime. Maybe it was the uniform and the look of venom in their eyes that made Dan feel no guilt surrounding their deaths.

He had no time to ponder it now. The light going out would have no doubt caused a disturbance and Dan did not want to be there when it was investigated. He promptly grabbed the remaining ammo from the cupboard, yanked the knife from where it lay in the man's chest, and headed for the door.

There was only one way up, which meant there was only one way down. So, when Dan looked out and saw the ladder was already being climbed, he had few other options. They saw him and tried to grapple for their weapons whilst clinging onto the ladder. Dan had the advantage. The watchtower was poorly designed. With cold eyes he drew his gun and fired three more shots. The bodies fell to the ground with each direct hit. His exit was now clear.

He slid down the ladder, saving precious time. The bodies at the bottom softened his fall. He climbed across them, gauging where to head next. The wall where the rest of the group had escaped seemed like the obvious choice – and that was exactly why he didn't want to use it. He needed an alternate route.

It was madness really. He knew it was as he climbed the drainpipe up the side of the warehouse. It was so odd to think that just a few weeks ago he was taking part in Elimination Day in that building. He had been fighting for the title of Supreme Cadet. He had been gaining the approval of his superiors. Now, he was throwing all that away. From the experience he took the skills they had taught him. The strength he had gained. The accuracy he had with a gun.

Dan was strong. He worked hard at it, every day. Working his body was something he forced himself to do each morning. He had never known why he was so adamant on keeping to his fitness schedule. Regardless, as he climbed the drainpipe and traversed the roof, he was grateful for his self-discipline.

The warehouse was perhaps one of the largest buildings in Camp Clandestine. Not the tallest – the dormitories were like skyscrapers – but it was large enough to hold aircrafts. He surveyed the area. Nobody had seen him climb. Everybody was still running about like headless chickens down below. There was a small group fussing over the body of a girl on the grass. Dan recognised her. She was the ginger one. The one who had started all this. They dragged her by the legs across the field. Her eyes were wide, empty. They hauled her over the wall.

Dan looked away. He couldn't bear to watch. He looked at the darkness of the night and felt the chill in the air. The breeze ruffled his dark hair, and his green eyes shone.

It had taken him some time, but he'd made his decision. He was a part of this now. There was no turning back.

He looked across at the wall closest to him. From where he stood on top of the warehouse, he could see right over it. There was nothing he could use to swing from, no tree to climb. But the wall was too high from him to traverse on his own. He needed help to get across it and didn't have the arms of a companion to haul him up. Instead he used the height of the building.

He gave himself a run up. He shook the fear from his head, and he sprinted as fast as he could. His feet pounded on the roof but didn't slip.

He reached the edge – and leaped.

CHAPTER TWO

That night was the darkest of Nia's life.

She walked with the others in an empty and echoing silence. The trees around them were barren and still. The further they got from Camp Clandestine, the quieter the darkness became. With each step, they left the restrictions behind them. They became freer. And yet not a single one of them had stopped to celebrate.

Nia could still see it in her head. She closed her eyes, and it was still there – burned onto the inside of her eyelids.

Bella had reached for her hand. They were so close. She was the last person left to reach the wall. Nia had been waiting to help her up. But Nia's outstretched palm had been splattered with Bella's blood. They had caught up with them. The group was a few seconds too late. A bullet had ripped through Bella's chest with such force that Nia didn't know what had happened, at first.

It was if the memory was muted. Nia had screamed and Bella had crashed to the floor, and the Authorities had dragged her rucksack from her. They had shouted, there were sirens, there were more gunshots. The sounds had echoed across the training field. Eddie had grabbed Nia from under the armpits, hauling her up the tree and over the wall, yelling about how they had to go – now.

But in Nia's memory it was all quiet. Everything had been silenced. The extreme intensity of the sounds had overwhelmed her. Especially when compared with the stillness in the forest that now surrounded them.

Veronika walked in front. She still had the beautiful scarf around her head like a bandana – vibrant purple and yellow dye securing her cornrows tightly out of her face. Amongst the darkness of the forest, and the colourless uniforms they wore, it was a beautiful contrast. Jay walked a few steps behind her. He kept brushing his dirty blonde curls from his forehead. His face was glistening with a thin layer of drying sweat.

Charles had his head low. The piece of hair that he often brushed out of his face was left to dangle. He still looked pale as ever. Nia wondered if he was hungry after vomiting earlier.

Eddie was trying his best to walk beside her. His face was hideously gnarled from where the tree had scratched it to pieces. He could barely see through his eye now. There was blood everywhere. It had trickled down his face and neck, and then dried there. Charles had his medical kit with him, but it was as if they had all forgotten. Their feet kept walking, as if moving without their permission.

They had been travelling for some time when Jay finally asked the question.

"So… what now?"

They all stopped and came naturally to somewhat of a circle. Eyes looked at one another in anticipation. In the end, they all landed on Nia.

She shook her head. "I don't know," she said, quietly.

"You don't know?" Charles said. "You didn't make a plan for when we got out?"

"We didn't actually know if we would get out," Eddie put in.

"Still – there's no idea of where to go?" Veronika asked. "What to do? A safe place to stay at least, whilst we figure the rest of it out?"

"I think you're forgetting something, Veronika," Nia said. "I did very little when it came to putting this plan together. It wasn't my idea to escape. This wasn't my plan–"

"Well whose was it then?"

"It was Bella's."

Everything went quiet again. Charles looked down at his feet.

"I just did as I was told," Nia continued. "I'm not the one

that got us out of there. She is. And she's the only one of us that didn't make it across that wall." She gulped back a sob. "We're all under a lot of stress. Tonight was… tough, to say the least. But I'm sorry – I don't know where we go from here."

"There'll be something we can do," Jay reassured her. He placed a hand on his cousin's shoulder. "Maybe we can find a cave – or some sort of shelter, at least. Just for tonight. We can deal with the rest of this revolution crap tomorrow, yeah?"

Everybody nodded. It would be nearing dawn soon. They needed to get some rest.

The group began to move forward again, their eyes peeled for a potential sleeping spot. Charles had the idea that sleeping out of reach might be best – if they could find a tree that had some sheltering leaves.

Jay held back for a second until Nia and Eddie caught up.

"Can I have a minute?" he asked her.

"Sure."

Jay looked at Eddie, who promptly took the hint. He went over to Veronika and Charles and they discussed the possibility that the trees in the distance were pines. They would have a decent amount of shelter – they didn't shed their needles through the winter.

"Are you okay?" Jay asked.

Nia pressed her lips together and her eyes got teary. "I don't think I've ever had a friend before," she said, "but Bella was probably the best friend there was."

"I'm so sorry, Nia."

"Don't be. It's not your fault. Bella wouldn't have wanted to die any other way." She laughed, but it didn't hold any humour behind it.

"She was a great leader."

"She really was." Nia smiled.

The two of them watched as Charles, Eddie and Veronika took it in turns to try and climb a tree. Charles wasn't tall enough to reach the lowest branch and lacked the agility skills to leap up for it. Veronika was the same height as him, and again struggled. Eddie gave her a leg up and she climbed the rest of the branches with minimal effort. They heard Charles curse Veronika's strength.

"She was inspiring, I think that's what it was," Nia said. "I was so terrified of the idea of being Curious. But then she came along and made me realise that being different and breaking the rules isn't so bad. She's the one that started all this. She spoke of changing the world, taking down the Government and the Dictator... I just don't know if that's possible without her."

Jay thought for a moment and readjusted his rucksack. "You think she's the reason we're all here?"

"Exactly."

"Nia, I didn't leave the camp tonight because of Bella." He looked at her. "I left because I trusted you. And because the idea of leaving my romantic future in the hands of the Marital Pairings Department makes me feel sick. I didn't know Bella. Sure, she inspired you and got you on board with this – but you inspired me. If it had been anybody else, I wouldn't have come. We've known each other since we were little kids – I trust you. We can do this. With or without Bella, we're not going to give up. She wouldn't have wanted that."

Nia nodded. "You're right. Of course, you're right."

"So, what's the plan, boss?" He nudged her with his elbow, playfully.

"Take down the Dictator." She smirked at him. "Change the fucking world."

CHAPTER THREE

Her body was so frail, it saddened him to see her like that. He hadn't known her well at all. Dan realised he hadn't ever said a word to her.

But he also realised she was the reason he was stood there. She was the reason he had crossed that wall. She was the reason he was free.

His arm was scratched and bleeding – the same arm with the gunshot wound through the hand. He had landed in a tree. He had aimed for it – he wanted to break his fall, not his legs, and he had succeeded. But his arm had snagged in the branches, and it was sprained, dislocated or broken. He wasn't sure.

But he fought the pain. Dan scooped her up and hauled her over his good shoulder.

He walked for miles. He didn't know which direction he was heading in. He stopped only when his legs gave way. After a day, he found a large pool of fresh water. Before taking a drop for himself, he washed the dirt from Bella's hands and the blood from her face. He made sure her eyes were closed.

The view was spectacular. Dan had never seen anything like it before. The water was so clear, and the sky, although sodden with potential rain, appeared higher, brighter. There was so much space. Dan had no idea where he was – and neither did anybody else. For the first time in his life he was entirely and utterly alone. The quiet felt loud, at first. But then he heard birdsong and the wind rustle the trees. He watched the breeze create ripples on the surface of the lake. The pain in his arm didn't cease, but the ache in his heart at being free – it pounded harder with each breath. He had made the right decision, coming here.

Over the course of several hours, he dug a hole. He placed

Bella inside and found a flower to place on her chest, to cover the wound. Dan covered her with dirt and found rocks to ensure that animals wouldn't dig her up. He wanted to create a sound resting place for her – to thank her for everything she had done for him, for them, and for the world.

He hunted a rabbit with his gun and ate the meat raw, having no means to light a fire. He washed in the lake and tended to his wounds. He popped his shoulder back into place. Dan could see himself staying there forever – but knew that it simply wasn't possible.

After a few days, he collected the things he had managed to scavenge: his gun, his rabbit pelt, and a full skin of water made from its stomach.

Dan placed a handful of wild foxgloves on the grave and knelt in front of her. He bowed.

Then he stood up and brushed off his knees. He headed into the forest.

He had work to do.

BOOKS BY THIS AUTHOR

Liberty

Clandestine

Calamitous (Coming Soon)